The Soul Loves Most
What Is Lost

Also by Paul S. Piper

Novels and Short Fiction

The Wolves of Mirr
South Fork & Other Stories

Poetry

Now and Then
Winter Apples
Dogs and Other Poems
And Light

Books of Essays (co-editor)

Father Nature
X Stories
A Flutter of Birds Passing through Heaven

The Soul Loves
Most What Is Lost

Paul S. Piper

BOOK VIEW CAFE
Book View Café
Las Vegas, NV

The Soul Loves Most What Is Lost
Paul S. Piper

Copyright ©2021 by Paul S. Piper
Book View Café, August 16, 2022
ISBN: 978-1-63632-054-0

Cover Design by Maya Bohnhoff
Production team:
Editor, Sara Stamey
Copyreader/proofreader, Sherwood Smith
Ebook formatter, Jennifer Stevenson
Print formatter, Marissa Doyle

This book is a work of fiction and all that entails.

Book ViewCafé
304 S. Jones Blvd. Suite #2906
Las Vegas NV 89107

www.bookviewcafe.com

The title is a line from the novel *All the Living* by C. E. Morgan

Dedication

This book is dedicated to all the Japanese internment victims, to my mother, Winnifred Ann Piper, who ventured to visit us while dying of cancer, and to my dear friend Bill Eleson who died of pancreatic cancer.

Part I

May 3

Yuki stared into her eyes in the mirror trying to catch the cancer staring out. It was tricky. Trapped in her wounded body, it was a serpent – poisoned, irradiated, withdrawn, and resting. But it would regain strength and it would strike back. She could see its flickering tongue. It would soon kill her.

How deep her eyes were, how unnerving, like amber and its depth in time. Far below the surface the serpent coiled. And surrounding her eyes and the serpent, a mask pale as mist. Months ago, her brittle hair had left her in clumps. She raised her thin arm and slid her hand over a bald, shiny head. Then she smiled. She had been taught long ago to smile even in tribulation, and it was a difficult habit to break. And she was always beautiful when she smiled.

The mirror stood on a small vanity of institutional plastic and stainless steel. To her immediate left stood a vase of mauve tulips, their petals stretched embarrassingly open. Under the vase was a small square note-card of thick ivory paper. On the card in black ink, in lovely script were the words "You can beat this. I'll be back next weekend. Love, Karen." Next to the tulips was a pile of envelopes, letters, emails, scribbled notes, and adjacent were two tubes of lipstick, various lotions, a lustrous black wig and iridescent orange and green bottles of pills.

The room was small and rectangular, but windows on the far wall opened onto a spacious well-groomed lawn, interrupted by an occasional towering Douglas Fir. Those trees were probably over one hundred and fifty feet tall the day I was born, thought Yuki. Such paltry things we are, except for our hubris. Life and death toy with us. We lose whatever nobility we've earned in their gaze.

Two crows strutted beneath the nearest tree, hunting in the pine needles for treasures, squawking at each other. Yuki watched them for a few minutes then turned away. She would be leaving tomorrow and she was scared. This home was a brief respite for her, and her journey beyond the front door was uncharted.

Memories came to her at random. If she tried to remember something, it was hopeless, but then, out of the blue, one came. But not always the one she wanted. And not always when she wanted. This memory came to her in a dream, and began with her running down a long hallway, her mother waiting at the far end, arms outstretched. But when she ran into her mother's arms they turned to dust and fell to the ground, and there was nothing there to grasp. Nothing tangible. And now was a different time, a loud pompous man orating, "To dust we shall return, we shall be turned to dust." Her arms were gone. Her mother was gone. She was alone in the long hallway, only the silence of the wood creaking, the shadows of footsteps redacting.

From down the hall, Yuki heard dinner plates

rattling on a metal cart, the cart's wheels rattling on the tile floor. First Carol Guterson, then Wendy Riordan, then Yuki, then Diane Faber, then Kitty Notely. The nightly feeding ritual. Heavy white plates covered with steel discs, a hole in the center to let out steam. Slices of tasteless turkey smothered in runny gravy, hyper-orange carrots, hyper-green peas, a carafe of tea, black, and a slice of cake edged with gummy pink tasteless frosting. Miho made sure to place a tsukemono on a small saucer.

Yuki always tried to eat it all. Another thing she had been taught that was difficult to forget. There were always lean times. But these days she largely failed and vomited it all up. The tea however, came after, and always soothed her.

How interesting, she thought, the way a life is constructed, most habits and tendencies taking root while a young child, learned from your parents. You carry them with you like gifts or curses your whole life. And then, in the liberation of death, they become irrelevant. You stare them down. You dissolve them.

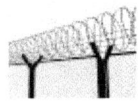

Yuki was seventy-two and both her parents were dead. Her mother had died eleven years ago at the age of eighty. She had related to her mother the way her daughter Alice related to her – on weekends and with irregular phone calls. Karma, they used to call it. Yuki had no right to bitch, but she laughed bitterly. If only we could retrieve the past like some old sweater we knitted, and redo the stitches.

Her father had died shortly after she'd begun classes at the University of Washington. A sudden massive heart attack while on his regular morning walk. Her father, Furuya Hiroto, or Hiroto Furuya as he began calling himself in America, had been a judge in Japan, but had left in 1932, the year Yuki was born on U.S. soil. Coming to America had been a matter of principle for her father, who she remembered as a moral and philosophical man, although his principles often left him inflexible. Hiroto felt his country was becoming dangerously expansive and bloated with hubris. He idealized America as a land of freedom and opportunity, just like the posters stated.

Once in America, Hiroto shunned everything Japanese. Moving from California to Seattle, he refused to settle in Japantown, and opted for lower Queen Anne. Luckily, he had brought money from Japan. He studied and took a job as a paralegal with an international law firm located on Fifth and Mercer. He courted white Americans for friends, and succeeded. Yuki's father was intelligent, amiable and generous.

It was almost a rule of law in the house not to speak Japanese, or to cook in the "old ways." Beef, potatoes, lettuce salad and ice cream, usually strawberry, replaced rice, tofu, fish, bok choy, tsukemono and miso soup. Chairs replaced tatami mats. Forks replaced chopsticks. Only Yuki's mother tried to remain traditional, ultimately obeyed Hiroto. She became American too.

Yuki remembered how disbelieving and stunned her father was when they were forced to go to the camps. Herded like cattle into the train at King Street

Station. Her father stated over and over to anyone who would listen that he was a patriot. He would go and fight for his country. Yuki remembered him being hit with a baton by a policeman whose sleeve he'd grabbed. She had been terrified, her father kneeling in the street, still holding the policeman's sleeve.

It was not until he was in camp, and finally offered the chance to assert his new American identity, that he declined. He was too old he said, and far too jaded by then. He refused to renounce his citizenship, however, as many Nisei did. The camp hadn't just scarred Hiroto and Yuki, it had shattered them and left them to put themselves back together.

She turned to the window again but the crows were gone. Shadows lengthened across the grass. She wanted to forget so much.

Her mother, Mizuki, had lived alone in her small bungalow in Kalispell, Montana, where she'd moved after Hiroto died. She lived there the remainder of her life and never moved back to Seattle. Her mother had died of a heart attack as well, cooking breakfast. Smoke from the burning pan alerted a neighbor. The family, what was left of it – a straggle of aunts, one daughter and cousins – buried her in a small hillside cemetery overlooking Flathead Lake. Yuki wondered if her mother could see the lake from where she lay? That was how she'd imagined it. When you died you were in the ground but also in the sky, and you could see everything. If the winds were up today, the whitecaps would break far off shore the way they had the day of the burial. Yuki had not cried at the funeral, but she had cried many times since.

She toyed with her peas.

Her doctor's visit, several months ago, had been a routine checkup. Some stomach problems Yuki had attributed to stress. What followed had been chaos that left her disoriented and weightless, as if she could blow away. After a barrage of tests, she'd been informed she had stage four pancreatic cancer. Stage four? She didn't know how to act. How many stages were there?

The GTX cycles had been the hardest. Gemzar, Taxotene, and Xeloda in five cycles over fifteen weeks. And then radiation, and her beautiful hair had left her. She hadn't wanted to see anyone, which made her friends more insistent to see her.

"This is not the time to push your friends away," Karen Pope told her, somewhat forcefully.

And then, after chemotherapy and radiation had savaged her, the doctors performed surgery, the Whipple procedure, named after the first man to slice out half the stomach, the gall bladder, head of the pancreas, duodenum, jejunum and adjacent lymph nodes. Pieces of her body removed. After the operation she wondered what they did with them? Toss them in the county dump? Sell them online for research? She had never experienced such pain as when she woke from that recent episode of her life. Pain killers became her best friend.

Tomorrow her daughter Alice would come and get her. Tomorrow was her last day of hyper-green peas.

Alice would deliver her from FirCrest Convalescent Home to her Queen Anne condo with its walls of glass and sweeping views of Elliot Bay, its abundance of orchids, her cat Kitso, and an inevitable mountain of mail, phone calls and email. Her post-operative stay at Fircrest had been arranged on her doctor's advice. Yuki, left to her own devices would have returned home immediately, and as soon as the pain was bearable drowned herself in work. But now she was thankful someone else had made the decision.

Although the stay at Fircrest was often frustrating and difficult, it had given Yuki time to think and reminisce, something she hadn't done in a long time. It had given her time to remember.

Even at seventy-two Yuki loved her work. She'd gotten into real estate after graduating from the University of Washington with an MBA in 1956. Before Seattle was anything but an amalgam of neighborhoods drained by the original skid road. Before Starbucks and Amazon and Microsoft and REI put it on the map in a big way.

Yuki was hired by Katherine Street Realty to do their books, and being bright, learned the ropes quickly. She liked people and getting out of the office, and soon the ledgers weren't nearly as appealing. She obtained her real estate license in 1959 and began what turned into a long and lucrative career, initially for Katherine Street, then for her own company.

"Mrs. Waldren?"

It was Miho poking her head around the corner of the room.

"Are you sleeping?"

"You always ask me if I am sleeping," replied

Yuki. "Am I ever sleeping?"

"Sometimes, but then you don't answer," Miho answered laughing. "How are you feeling?"

"Like I've been hit by a truck and dragged for miles."

"So, you want pain medicine?"

"Yes, and a sleeping pill and some tea."

"You want some tea. Ahh, you must be feeling better. Tea before bed."

"I'm feeling okay, actually."

"You're going home tomorrow."

"Yes."

"Exciting."

Yuki said nothing. She was going home to die.

Miho returned in a few minutes with a small paper cup containing two pills.

"Thank you, Miho. I'll miss you."

Miho bowed. "I'll miss you too." She stood smiling, seeming to not want to leave. "You will get better, Mrs. Waldren. You'll see." Then after a minute, "I'll get your tea."

Yuki nodded and smiled herself, watching Miho back out of the room. Miho was the only Japanese woman working at Fircrest, and they'd instantly bonded. Although Miho was not assigned to Yuki, she always checked on her in the evening. They both knew evening was the most vulnerable time of day.

She didn't want to contradict Miho with what doctor Wyalet had said after surgery, now three weeks past.

"I'm going to be blunt, Yuki, I'm not going to sugar coat it. Pancreatic cancer is almost always fatal. You could have six months, or maybe only two. It could even be sooner. Toward the end things will be rough, but we'll put you in hospice so the pain will be controlled." He stood over her tapping his clipboard. He is a kind man, thought Yuki, despite his demeanor. He must hate telling people this. "Put your affairs in order. And of course, if you're inclined, pray for a miracle."

Miho returned with tea.

"Too hot," she said laughing, setting it on the bedside table, Yuki already starting to drift.

Miho bowed again. "Bye, Mrs. Waldron."

Yuki opened her eyes and spoke very softly. "Goodbye Miho. And thank you."

The heavy metal door clicked shut. Yuki lay back and closed her eyes again. She took several deep breaths, then grimacing sat up, and swung her legs over the side of the bed. It was Miho's gift to her. She would drink the tea, even though it was too hot.

May 4

ALICE WAS THERE TO pick Yuki up at 10:30 the following morning, but had to wait in the lobby for some paperwork to get squared away. She was on her cell phone when Yuki entered the spacious lobby, an attendant walking behind her wheeling Yuki's single bag. Alice was gesturing with her left arm and Yuki could see she was irritated. Alice, like Yuki of yesteryear, hated to wait. She glanced over and saw her mother, waved, forced a good-bye, and snapped the phone shut. Then, staring at her mother, pushed a smile through her frustration.

"Hey mom." Alice walked over and kissed Yuki's cheek. "How are you feeling?"

"A hair better than when I came in." She looked Alice up and down and was proud. "Thanks for coming. I hope I didn't hold you up too long. There was a lot of paperwork."

"Always is. You look good."

"Hah! Don't *you* start."

Alice took her bag and began walking out the entrance, then stopped suddenly and turned. "Are you okay to walk?"

"I'm okay." Yuki smiled.

And then she struck out, one foot in front of the other. It was the farthest Yuki had walked in weeks, and after a few yards she felt unsteady. But she stopped and watched Alice, walking ahead of her, sashaying her hips side-to-side, powering her legs, moving forward in the world. Yuki studied her. If she was to succeed, she'd need to be like that.

"I have a doctor's appointment Tuesday, but don't worry, I'll take a cab." It was a test, one of many that's given to child, to parent, to whoever is in power.

"Mom, don't be like that. You know I can drive you."

"I think they have a shuttle."

"Mom...!" Alice shook her head. "I can take you. Just let me know when you need to go, and I'll schedule it in."

"You're so busy."

"Mom." They'd reached the end of the walk and Alice took her hand. "Mom," she said again. "You need help off the curb?"

"No, I'm okay. Better than okay." They walked together for several yards, then Yuki suddenly doubled up laughing. The world was SO funny. Everything!

"Are they giving you drugs, Mom?"

"I...hope...so."

"Don't get any weird ideas, Mom." Alice was shaking her head, smiling. "You're just dreaming."

Yuki heard the sing-song ring of a cell phone, heard Alice say "damn," and reach into her purse. Yuki watched her study the phone, stare at the caller's number, then let it ring.

"I'm supposed to be in a meeting now."

"I'm sorry to be a burden, honey."

"You're not a burden, Mom. Jeeez. Stop doing that."

"Doing what?"

"You know. Don't play innocent on me. Here, this one." Alice stopped in front of a white BMW.

"Did you get a new car?"

"It's Franklin's. Mine's in the shop. It's a long, not-very-interesting story."

Alice opened the door for Yuki and popped the trunk, lifting Yuki's bag and setting it in. "You don't have much in here, do you?" she said, getting into the car. "You travel light."

Yuki said nothing, staring out the window as Alice pulled away from the curb and began driving down 50th. After several minutes Yuki began talking. "The trees are beautiful out here. It's so sunny. I couldn't open the window there you know. In the Fircrest." She began laughing again. "It was several acres surrounded by maple trees! This is practically the first fresh air I've tasted in over a week."

"Couldn't you walk outside? I'm sure a nurse could have taken you."

"I've been very tired."

They drove in silence for a few minutes, Alice expertly merging onto I-5, threading the lanes, then merging into the carpool lane. Yuki saw her shoulders relax.

"So, Mom, what did they tell you?"

"I have pancreatic cancer."

"I *know* that Mom!! What did they say? About treatment? About recovery?"

"The doctor told me I have six months. Probably less."

"That bastard! He said that? He has no right to say that." Alice glared her way through traffic.

"It's true, honey. I don't have much time. The cancer has spread significantly. Those were his words."

"They don't know. They just guess. You've got to be optimistic. Positive. Positive thoughts have a lot of power."

Yuki stared out the window. The colors were brighter than she remembered.

"How do you feel? Are you in a lot of pain?" Alice blew a strand of hair off her forehead.

"Sometimes. It seems to flare up randomly. I was really tired until they started the prednisone. That was four days ago. It gives me energy."

"Good." She fished around in her purse and found a pack of gum and held it out to her mom. "Here. Juicy Fruit. Your favorite. You look skinny. Not eating, huh?"

Yuki took the pack and slid one out, unwrapped it and placed it slowly into her mouth. She could just make out its sweetness, but the taste of the gum she'd loved since she was a kid was gone. She handed the pack back to Alice. "I'm not very hungry anymore, and sometimes when I do eat, I get sick. They gave me some new pills that might help."

"You should get some marijuana. That's supposed to help with appetite and nausea."

"That's all I need. To become a pothead at seventy-two."

Alice shifted lanes and exited Aurora on Queen Anne. "Almost home."

"How's Kitso?"

"Kitso's fine. Desperate for attention. Clawing all your furniture apart."

"The orchids?"

"Fine. I've been misting them every day. Everything's fine, Mom. Mail's in, newspaper is canceled but will start up tomorrow, message machine overflowing and blinking." Alice took her eyes off traffic and glanced at her mother. "Don't do too much, Mom."

Yuki laughed. Her laugh had lightness in it. What can I do?"

Alice wound higher on the north side of Queen Anne onto Third, then Bigelow, and Highland, finally pulling to the curb in front of an older well-kept sand-colored brick building with white trim. Initially apartments, the units had been condo-ized and Yuki had gotten in on the first round.

"I'd come in but I have this meeting. Will you be okay?"

Yuki laid her hand on Alice's arm, on her fine arm-hair like so many tiny brush strokes. This woman who had been her baby, her child, was now evolving into being her guardian.

"I'm okay. I'll be fine." Yuki leaned over and kissed her quickly on the cheek, then unclipped her seatbelt and got out. She felt extremely dizzy but didn't let Alice see it.

"You okay, Mom?"

Yuki nodded, holding tightly onto the handle of her luggage.

"I'll call you," Alice yelled after her gunning the car out into the street.

The yard was meticulously landscaped and maintained, the bark mulch and pea gravel raked and picked free of debris, and the huge pink-blossomed rhododendron roseum were just beginning to drop petals as if saying goodbye to spring. Chickadees were arguing in the branches of a maple.

Yuki punched a number into the keypad and unlocked the front door. She checked her mailbox, empty, and let herself into the main lobby, its tiled floor a worn brocade of roses on a backdrop of what could only be snow. She pushed the elevator UP button, and stood leaning against the wall as it descended with its familiar clunking and scraping. She was very tired. She'd lived in bed for six days in the hospital after surgery then was moved by ambulance to Fircrest.

The heavy worn ornamental brass doors of the elevator opened and Yuki stepped in. It seemed like a long time since she'd put her jogging shorts and sneakers on for a run through Queen Anne. She pushed the top button, floor five, her home for the past twenty-eight years, and sank against the elevator wall.

Well, it didn't smell, so she had to give credit to Alice for emptying the garbage. The orchids, hoyas and other assorted plants looked dry but healthy. She'd told Alice that under-watering was better than over-watering.

She sat heavily on the pink sofa next to the phone and its insistent blinking light. Next to the phone lay a notepad with a page of scribbled messages. Surprisingly, she could pick out some of her letters in Alice's notes. The way she wrote her Rs and Ss, the loop on her Ls.

Kitso came bounding out of the bedroom when she heard her name. The cat leapt lightly onto Yuki's lap and began kneading her leg, purring loudly.

"You I've missed the most, Kitso," she said, stroking the long white fur along her spine, feeling the notches between each vertebra. The cat ate constantly and never gained an ounce. A doctor friend of hers had once recommended she donate Kitso to science so they could use her for weight loss research. Kitso rubbed her head against Yuki's chin, and Yuki found herself crying softly.

"What am I going to do dear kitty? What does one do when they know they will die soon?"

The questions hung, clouds in the sky of the room. The sky outside was pure azure.

Yuki picked a photo of herself as new graduate from UW off the shelf. She'd stood in her robe with three leis around her neck, her eyes shining despite the gray day. A young woman full of hope and optimism. She tipped the photo, firing it with sun, immolating herself. Then erupting in anger, heaving the photo across the room where it shattered against the wall.

"I will never be her again. Fuck her!"

A book of yoga asanas followed. It hit the wall so hard it broke the spine of the book. The phone and answering machine followed, tearing the cord from the wall. Then couch pillows, a table lamp, and a glass that failed to shatter. Another glass. Yuki collapsed in a crying heap on the sofa. Kitso, who'd leaped from her lap at first hint, watched her from the kitchen doorway, startled but patient.

Yuki woke, not knowing how long she'd slept. Her cheeks felt crusty with dried tears. She still burned with anger. The hopeless ridiculousness of the whole thing.

Cancer!! How dare they!! How dare God!! What right? This was her life and it was being taken away, not instantly, but piece by piece until the vital piece, the one that ticked, the one that had the essence of "her" in it, was withdrawn. And then? Blackness? Nothingness? Heaven or hell?

"Naahh!" Yuki exclaimed, standing up. She picked up her purse, which had escaped being heaved across the room, and wobbled into the kitchen, grasping the counter like a life raft. Orchids greeted her in their bay window home, colorful faces on their long, slender Modigliani necks. Who will take care of my orchids? Who will take care of Kitso? Several dishes were dry in the drainer. Outside the wires strung along the alley looked momentarily like barbed wire.

Yuki tipped her purse onto the table and poured out bottles of fluorescent green, orange, and red, each jammed with pills. She picked up the bottles and arranged them in a row. Prednisone, Xanax, Ambien, Somastatin, Immodium, Methylprednisone, Ducoalx, Oxycontin. Six months ago, she took nothing except a one-a-day vitamin. And now this. She stared at the bottles and thought them oddly beautiful as they caught the morning sun. Then anger swarmed her again, and she swept the bottles from the table, her arms like frantic wings. Then it was over.

She felt energy drain from her, and holding onto the sink, took a glass from the dish drainer and filled it with water. She always drank a lot of water, but now it seemed more precious than ever. She held the glass to her lips, wet them, then tipped it back and swallowed until the glass was empty. Each swallow was painful, but pain had become synonymous with life.

Funny how it takes staring into certain death to make the world precious. She set the glass down, watching how it reflected the room as an inward curve, the edges disappearing into darkness. "Even in clarity is darkness." Where did she read that? She used to read so much when Mel, her husband, was alive, before she became so busy, before now.

Yuki walked cautiously over and picked up the bottles, arranging them as she'd set them, then returned to the living room and began cleaning up her wreckage. Pouring herself another glass of water, she settled into the couch and began sorting through a pile of mail, separating it into junk and anything worth reading – that pile containing a number of card-sized envelopes, that once opened would wish her back to good health and cheer; the other pile everything else. She didn't have the heart to open the best-wishers just now. Rather, she tackled the bills with vigor, writing checks, making notes in her book, numbers in columns, expanding spreadsheets, becoming lost in it.

Yuki finished the bills, then ran a shower.

Braced against the wall, she let the water cascade over her. Like baptism, she would now start anew. Each moment new. That had been a Buddhist teaching. It came to her out of her past like a butterfly. She felt her life becoming more permeable. The past was no longer in boxes in a cellar or attic somewhere. It was in the air.

After drying herself, she slipped into a turquoise silk Kimono her mother had given her, one of two Yuki now owned. Many people had given her kimonos over the years, including Mel, but this gift she'd kept. Like her father, Yuki had strongly rejected being Japanese, wanting almost desperately at times to fit into the dominant culture. America. The USA.

When her father died, her mother had slowly slipped back into her old cultural habits. After moving to Montana, she had worn kimonos regularly, and cooked Japanese dishes for her neighbors, who found her "charming." She had added a dimension of culture that was sorely missing from the Flathead Valley.

May 4, Evening

LATER THAT EVENING, AFTER she'd sprayed, watered, and fertilized the orchids, fed the cat, showered again, feeling dirty, then napped, Yuki ate some frozen shrimp she thawed and sautéed with wilting peapods, celery and broccoli. Staring back at her, lost on a huge plate, the food looked, what? And the shrimp with their beady eyes, staring at her, daring her, and then…? Tasteless and rubbery.

The word "lost" drifted into her mind, then out, taking her with it, and her mind was suddenly empty, a courtyard of rock, and a cold itinerant wind began licking, searching, and sniffing the edges.

She knew the chemo had killed her taste buds, trimming them like so much unwanted shrubbery. The nurses had told her that she could taste salt, but everything else would be flat. To test the theory, she opened a box of expensive truffles her friend Carmen had given her. She bit into one and watched a caramel-colored cream flow out. She sucked on it and could taste a bit of salt and distorted sweetness. Nothing else. No caramel, no walnut, no luscious Belgium chocolate. She set the chocolate onto the saucer and picked up her tea. Only the heat of tea pleased her.

She drifted.

A sudden three knocks, followed by another two.

As soon as she'd arrived home Yuki had wondered when she would have to confront Bill. At seventy-nine, courting Alzheimer's, her neighbor Bill, William Corbett III, had been courting her since his wife died four years ago. Yuki enjoyed his company, but harbored no romantic intentions. Bill, she thought, was by now acting on confused instinct alone. Though usually sweet, his moods were beginning to swing erratically.

"Come in," she called softly, but knew he would anyway if the door was unlocked. If locked, he would knock again, often for a long time, then go away.

Bill was a tall distinguished man with a white mane swept back in the regal fashion of Confederate generals. He was dressed, as usual, impeccably, in pleated sand-colored twill pants and a royal blue cashmere sweater over a white turtleneck. His choice of shoes was always tasseled loafers. A colonel in the army, Bill had never lost his military bearing. He walked up to Yuki and took her hand.

"How are you, dear? How have the wolves of medicine been treating you?"

"Sit down, Bill. You're blocking my view." She smiled.

Bill turned, and catching the evening lights of Seattle fanned out like a frozen sparkler below them commented, "It is lovely isn't it?" He settled himself on the couch a few feet away from her and she handed him her cup of tea. It was their ritual, to share cups, plates, even silverware.

"You look thin. Are you eating properly?"

"I'm not hungry for much." As she voiced it, Yuki realized the implications went far beyond food.

"You don't have anything contagious, do you dear?"

"I have cancer, Bill. Pancreatic cancer."

"Oh." He nodded sadly. "Damn." He had forgotten. It was like this with Bill. In and out. Then talking too loudly, as if she couldn't hear well, "I've heard of your doctor, Doctor Wyalet. He's a *bastard*, if I must say it."

Yuki said resignedly, "He's just doing his job."

Bill sipped the tea then set the cup down on the saucer next to the bleeding truffle. "May I?"

"Take it."

Bill picked up the truffle and finished it in one bite. "Ahh, that's good." He smacked his lips. "I used to eat chocolate like this all the time when I was stationed in Munich. I have told you about Munich, haven't I?"

"Yes. Bill."

Yuki stared out the window wishing now Bill hadn't come, that she'd locked the door and stayed quiet. Her eyes strayed to a photo of her parents in traditional Shinto garb. One of the few things left after the war ended, when they returned. to Seattle, were four boxes in a friend's closet. The remnants of their previous life, before the camp. When her mother moved to Montana, she'd been insistent that Yuki take the photo.

"I can't believe we gave it up so easily," she'd said, inferring that they had adopted Christianity too facilely, or for the wrong reason. "But you give up things when you move half-way around the world.

You make sacrifices, you grow a new life. You *have* to."

"It doesn't look good, does it, Yuki?" Bill interrupted her memory.

"No Bill, I am going to die soon." Her voice fell off the word.

"It doesn't look good. But," Bill stretched out his legs and leaned back, "if you want to talk about it, I'll listen. I'm a good listener, you know."

Yuki smiled in spite of herself.

"I know, Bill. I know. I know you." She knew she didn't want to say a word, but began talking anyway. "I can feel it in me. It's a presence, almost like pregnancy. It's feeding off me, Bill, and soon it will exhaust its food. I've met it in my dreams. I've talked to it. I've questioned it. Oh, I asked it the usual clichés. Why me? Why now? But it just grins at me. It won't answer me, and to tell you the truth I don't blame it. I don't even know why I'm asking these stupid questions. We are born. We grow and live and then we die. There are no answers. There are only stupid questions."

Bill shuffled his feet uncomfortably. "No Yuki, there are no answers." He scratched his nose. "My wife died you know."

"I know, Bill. I'm sorry. I don't mean this to be only about me. I know you've suffered too."

"And I have my disease."

"I know Bill, but at least they haven't given you a death sentence."

Bill coughed into his curled fist. "Some days I wish they had. Do you have any wine?"

"There's some Chardonnay in the fridge, but I'm not supposed to drink while taking these medications."

Bill laughed heartily. He had such a rich, deep laugh.

"They tell you that you will die soon, but don't drink with the medication." He began laughing really hard then, and it was contagious. "What's it going to do? Kill you?" He was shouting now.

Yuki wept with laughter. It all seemed so absurd.

"So, what do you want? Wine? Or do you want me to go back to my place and get something nice? A cognac or a Scotch?"

Yuki was still laughing too hard to answer. She was straying toward hysteria. Something about to break open.

May 7

I dreamt of an Arctic last night, an Arctic without life, only sculpted ice and blowing snow; black air and stars. At first I wandered, taking it all in. I was dazzled like a child. Then I became scared. The wind erased my tracks and I could no longer return to where I'd been. Then the cold froze any will or intention and I decided to lie down in the snow. I knew if I did this I would be erased. I would lose my life, my history, and I wanted that so badly. I took off my clothes and lay down in the snow. I tried to become numb, to lose myself, but everywhere I looked there I was. I could not escape this fever.

May 7, 7:34 a.m.

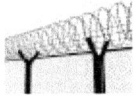

It was someone her friend and co-worker Allison Hart had recommended. A "Bereavement Counselor," she'd called him.

"My mother and sister both went to him after my father died. He's amazing."

And now his name, Raymond Sturgis, scripted on a gold-leaf panel glued to a teak door on the sixteenth floor of the Rowan Building off Fifth and Seneca.

Yuki had tried driving but felt dizzy looking over her shoulder while trying to back the Volvo out of the underground garage, so she'd called a cab. The cabbie had helped her out of the back, telling her to take care. For a moment the traffic, noise and blur of downtown Seattle was too much and she thought she might faint, but the feeling passed with a brace of salt air off Elliot Bay.

She stepped into an empty waiting room with a sofa and three chairs. Soft jazz streamed from hidden speakers, and an adjacent door, also teak, was closed. A photograph of two women laughing hung on one wall, and a painting of an orchard in pink blossom above a lake hung on the other. Yuki figured from the décor and location that bereavement counseling paid as well or better than real estate. She hung her apricot leather coat, took a seat and pulled a magazine from a glass holder. *Country Living.* She began paging through it at random until she heard the faint stir of voices and the inner door opened.

"Goodbye David. I'll see you next week at the same time." The man who spoke these words was in his sixties, wore his white hair semi-long, and had brilliant blue eyes.

"Okay. See you then." His client, also a man, wore a Brooks Brother's suit, and exited through the office avoiding Yuki's gaze.

"Hi. You must be Mrs. Waldren?" The man extended his hand, which Yuki took. It felt warm, like comfort, and for a second Yuki allowed herself to hope.

"I'm Doctor Raymond Sturgis. Come into my office."

Yuki followed him. His office was small and intimate, and the walls were adorned with Audubon prints.

Dr. Sturgis noticed her staring.

"I'm an amateur bird-watcher, so when I can't be outside…well. Besides, Audubon was a wonderful artist." Sturgis laughed. "Don't get the wrong idea though. They're prints."

"I know. The originals are at the New York Historical Society. I saw them once." She remembered going there with Mel, how he didn't want to leave, his face animated like a little boy's over the beauty of the birds. She was suddenly filled with sorrow.

"Lucky. I still haven't been there yet. Well, why don't you sit down?"

Yuki hesitated.

"Which chair should I take?"

"Anywhere you wish. You can even sit at the desk, but I'll require you to do my write-ups." Dr. Sturgis smiled and Yuki saw his laugh lines catch the soft light. He had a nice face, weathered and kind. Like someone's favorite grandfather in an L.L. Bean catalog.

There was a small desk with a computer at the far end of the room, a loveseat, a wooden rocking chair, Shaker-style, and a worn rose chaise lounge. Yuki chose the loveseat, and folded her legs under her. Dr. Sturgis sat in the lounge and leaned back.

"I'm glad you left me my favorite chair. It will get

things off to a good start." He laughed. It was an easy laugh. He was comfortable with this, whatever would come up. She could tell.

"So, what can I help you with, Mrs. Waldren? Or should I call you Yuki?"

"Yuki is fine." Yuki paused, pursed her lips then spoke. She felt like she was pushing words out into the air, freeing them.

"My doctors tell me that I'm going to die soon."

"Do you believe them?" He moved toward her rather than away.

"I don't want to, but I do."

"How do you feel about that?" Raymond Sturgis did not beat around the bush.

"When the medication is working, the dope, I'm in denial. But that's rare. The rest of the time I'm either in shock, afraid, depressed, or angry as hell."

"Yuki. Please look up. Look at me. Talk to me."

Yuki raised her head. "I'm not sure what to do. What am I supposed to do? There is so much inside me. It's so…I feel like I'm going to explode. Then I look around and the sun still brightens the rhododendron leaves, kids are still running and chasing each other, lovers still hold hands. It's so inconceivable that all this can go on, and I can end. It terrifies me." She stared at him hopelessly, then lowered her face in embarrassment.

Dr. Sturgis leaned back in his chair and closed his eyes. Yuki, looking up now, watched his nostrils dilate and compress. Then he spoke.

"There's no guide, Yuki, no textbook. It's a personal journey into uncharted terrain." He tipped the chair forward and opened his eyes. Yuki could see they were moist, compassionate, despite their brilliance. "Are you religious? Do you have beliefs that will help you?"

She spoke softly. "No. I gave it all up long ago. My parents came from Japan and were Shinto, but converted to Protestantism here. I was raised Protestant but gave it up. My husband Mel, he died a while back, was fascinated with Zen Buddhism. Some friends of his parents had learned it from an early monk, Sokei-an, who was living in Seattle. He was always bemused by my lack of interest."

"Why?"

"He thought I should be attracted to Zen, being Japanese and all."

"Hmmm."

"I have no religious beliefs. I'd rather not talk about it anymore."

Raymond stared at her for a minute or so without talking, and Yuki, strangely, felt like a child who'd been deceptive, and whose deceit was transparent.

"Okay. So why have you been told you will die soon?"

"I have cancer. Pancreatic cancer."

"I'm sorry. That's a nasty call. How long do they say you have?"

"Six months, but probably much less." Yuki talked softly, stared at the wall above Dr. Sturgis' head where a waxwing picked at a clump of yellow berries.

"Well, one thing I like to tell my patients, and it usually sounds like utter bullshit until they really digest it, is that this could be the best time of your life." He stopped but Yuki sat stoically. "And the reason is simple. There is no longer any pressure on you to maintain the facades or routines that trap you. You have been given a death sentence, true," Dr. Sturgis steepled his fingers, "but you have also been liberated. You can speak your mind and act in accordance with your heart. Your work now is to examine yourself, see what you can let go of, and where that will lead you."

"I need help." She closed her eyes.

"That's what I'm here for. Why don't you tell me about yourself? Who you are, where you grew up, some of your real accomplishments, your fears? Just start talking."

Yuki sat frozen for minutes, then abruptly stood. "This isn't working."

"Okay, what do you want to do?"

"I think I'll leave now."

"I'll tell you what. Why don't you go back into the waiting room and sit for a few minutes? If you feel like leaving after that, take off. But if you feel that I can be of some use, some help, come back in. I'll wait in here."

Yuki half-stood above the chair, motionless, then fell back into it and began crying. Dr. Sturgis stood and walked over to her with a box of tissues that was sitting on his desk. He hugged her shoulders and handed her a tissue.

"There, there. Take one of these. It will help."

It took a minute, but Yuki reached out and took it.

"Sometimes it's only the little things that can cover the big," Dr. Sturgis said, returning to his chair. Then very gently he said, "Now what do you want to tell me?"

"I was raped." Yuki spoke so quietly it was like a

branch brushing the window with shadow.

"When?"

"When I was a little girl. Twelve years old. I was in an internment camp in Idaho. My family, most of my friends, all Japanese, were moved from Seattle to Minidoka, Idaho. It was where they sent the Japanese during World War Two. They considered us traitors.

"One night two men, guards, took turns raping me and holding me down. They covered my mouth. I could barely breathe. One of them was an older man, and one was younger. They told me they'd kill me if I ever told anyone. They'd kill me and throw me into the river and no one would care. Everyone hated the Japanese since what happened at Pearl Harbor." The words flowed out of her.

"I never told anyone, not even my mother, not even my husband. I burned my clothes. I went home to Seattle a year later. I lived my life. And I never told anyone. But I never healed." She began crying again, holding her knees together, rocking. She talked to the floor.

"This single event has haunted me and controlled my entire life. I want to….I want to let this go. I want to die without feeling this shame." Her face was flushed, her heart beat like quick wings.

"I have a friend, a woman, who can help you with this."

"No, I'm here now. Try to help. You try to help." She stopped rocking, straightened and wiped her dripping nose. "What if it wasn't a rape? What if it was something else? How do you get people to let go of things that haunt them? To make things right before they die?"

Doctor Sturgis got up and crouched in front of her, not reaching out to her but letting her know he was there.

"Yuki, there is no one way. Everyone is different. Everyone has different needs. We work with what you have, what you need to do, and how you need to do it."

"I can't believe I told you. I haven't ever told anyone. Not my mother, not my husband. And now?"

"You weren't dying before, Yuki. Death does strange things for people. It's very liberating."

She wiped at her tears. "That seems like a silly thing to say, but it's true isn't it. There's no need to hold onto things."

"No, you're right, Yuki. That's a very important basic lesson about death. Many people don't even get that far. But death will take what you have. It will take your body, it will take your mind, your emotions, your possessions. There is no use holding on. Death will take what you have."

May 8

THE NEXT DAY YUKI called her friend David Oshiro, a Japanese-American man seven years younger. She had known David for twenty years. He was one of her most trusted friends.

"Come over," said David, "I was just making a little brunch."

David lived in a spacious loft off Belltown where he painted giant flowers that he sold in galleries worldwide. Yuki had found the place for him when Belltown was still a sketchy area of downtown, and David, moving to Seattle from San Francisco, and possessing a solid inheritance from his father's restaurant business, had bought the entire three-story building – an old carpet warehouse. Over the years David had converted it to apartments that he managed. He'd kept the top floor a loft. The walls were awash with light from huge windows, which enlivened large sensuous flowers painted directly onto the walls. To the right of the entrance there was a small kitchen and dining nook. David had been destined to become a chef before art kidnapped him, and whatever he was cooking probably smelled delicious, although Yuki's sense of smell was mute.

He gave her a kiss on the cheek, which she returned.

"You look good, considering. How do you feel?"

"Up and down. I had a rough day yesterday but today is a bit better. I'm on some heavy steroids. I think I could eat something. Many days I have no appetite." She began looking through a pile of books on the counter. Books on art, philosophy and cooking.

"Good. I'm making your favorite. A smoked salmon omelet with Stimson cheese and chives. It will be ready in a minute. Have a seat."

"This from the man who used to put broccoli and coffee in the blender." She laughed. David in his studio always made her feel light.

"Still do." He flashed her a beatific smile.

Yuki pulled out a chair and sat at the small worn wooden table.

The view that once overlooked Elliot Bay had been eclipsed by a row of condos. Yuki stared out the window and thought about time. Those condos were only a cloud blocking the view. Someday the cloud would move on. We all move on and leave what we may. David whistled as he cooked. He looked so youthful. She felt suddenly very glad she had called a cab and come over.

He set a plate in front of her, interrupting her musings. Steam rose from the eggs and enticed her. David set a sturdy glass of orange juice next to the plate. Then he set a place for himself.

He pointed as he took a large bite of omelet. "I've had that glass for over thirty years. I stole it from one of my dad's restaurants, can't remember which one. It's perfect for orange juice and ice water. Ever notice how some glasses just suck? They feel wrong, and others feel right for certain things? With that one it's ice water and orange juice. Nothing else."

Yuki smiled and picked up the glass. Whatever David said was always perfect. There had been a time when she thought of leaving her husband for him. That was until she realized how foolish that would be, what it would do to their friendship, and how valuable their friendship was.

"Thanks David."

He laughed. "For what? An omelet?"

"All this." She waved her hands to encompass the room.

"So, talk to me. How are you?"

Yuki looked across the room wistfully.

"Sometimes, sometimes I know. Sometimes it is very concrete. I actually collapse on the couch or the floor or wherever. I imagine myself buried by an avalanche or buried alive. But then I have no strength, no strength to fight, to dig, so I begin to let go."

"Are you afraid?"

"No. Something very strange happens. I relax and begin to breathe deep, and I feel something, sun maybe, flooding my body, and it's as if the snow suddenly melted. I'm free, and I stretch, and get to my feet and go on."

"You're a fighter, Yuki."

"I went to a bereavement counselor yesterday."

"Oh?" David raised his eyebrows.

"I think it was" she hesitated a moment, "good. I told him something I've never told anyone, something I've tried unsuccessfully to erase from my life."

"You never told me?" David showed mock

surprise and laughed.

"I never told my parents, my husband, my daughter. Not you or any of my friends. And now it seems foolish that I never did. I was afraid, ashamed, but now I'm not."

"What is it?"

"When I was young, I was in the internment camp in Idaho during the war."

"You've told me this. My father and mother also were. In Minidoka. My parents were in Manzanar."

"While in the camp I was raped by two of the guards. I was traumatized, and threatened with death if I told anyone."

"My God, Yuki! What did you do?"

"Nothing. I tried to forget. For my whole life I've tried to forget. So what is the first damn thing I tell that counselor?" She laughed, startling herself. "It was like a confession I've been waiting to tell my whole life."

"You felt shamed."

"I still do. But I let the genie out of the bottle, and you know what? Now I feel pissed."

"Take it from me, pissed is much better than ashamed. There must be something you can do. Some war crimes have charges. Is it too late to file charges? I mean these abused kids I read about in the *Times* are always filing charges against priests that savaged them when they were young. I don't see much difference."

"It was a long, long time ago, David. And the men were older. They're probably dead."

David sat back and sipped his coffee. "I don't know what to say, Yuki. I'm shocked. Profoundly, and saddened. What kind of animal would do that to a little girl? And they considered us savages." He made a spitting sound. "War. Why are we so fucked up?"

Yuki picked up the perfect orange juice glass and took a drink.

"You haven't touched your eggs, Yuki."

She picked up a forkful, put it in her mouth and chewed slowly. She tried to taste them but could only feel their warmth and the slippery, gooey texture of the cheese.

"Who were they? Do you know their names? Maybe we could find them. Maybe they're not dead." David leaned forward, trying to catch her eye. She was gaunt and her color washed, but she was still beautiful. He thought of her suddenly as a beautiful ghost.

"They're probably all dead by now. And I don't really care." But she knew that was a lie.

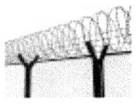

That afternoon Yuki sorted through the new mail of endless flyers and catalogs, then used a knife to slit open a letter from her cousin, Miki, who lived in the forest outside of Salem, Oregon. Miki was the only cousin Yuki still kept in touch with. The other, Michiko, had gone back to Japan.

Sweetest Yuki -

We are over-run with newts, and slugs are devouring the lettuce. Andrew is getting over a bad cold, but it's finally getting warm.

I hope you are not in too much pain, not too sick. My friend Justin has pancreatic cancer and has outlived all predictions. He eats nothing but raw foods, which you should look into (lots of information on the web) also laetrile, which is also called amygdaline, and is in apricot pits. And Justin refuses to do any more chemo or radiation. Here's his phone number – 503-236-8465. You should call him and talk. He has a lot of information that he says the medical community doesn't want you to know. They like their little monopoly. Anyway, call him!

Benny's down in the shop trying to get the Triumph up and running for a rally this weekend, and after that we're thinking of spending four or five days on the coast. It would be fun if you could join us. Let me know.

Love always,
Miki

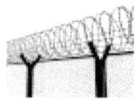

Yuki sat down at her computer. To her left was a cluster of photographs, all of her daughter and her late husband Mel. She ritually visited each of them: Mel and Alice on top of Mount Rainier; Alice on a dogsled; Mel fishing the south fork of the Stilliguamish; Mel and Alice standing on the float of a plane, laughing. Alice growing up, Mel getting older.

Mel had a narrow, freckled face, sandy hair that thinned noticeably over the course of the photographs, while Alice ranged from four years of age to nineteen, from cute to flirtatious, her hair longer in each photo. At sixteen they'd lost her for a few years.

She thought she hated them and wanted to see Japan for herself, outside the confines of a few regulated family vacations. The last photo was taken by a stranger on a street in New York. The three of them linking arms, laughing. Alice had come home to them a young woman. After touching the photos with her eyes, she lingered on a photograph of Mel.

His head, thrown back laughing, was framed by a lustrous sky, and behind him the snow-capped peaks of the Northern Cascades. It always cheered her, and gave her a sense of the spaciousness Mel carried with him.

She remembered when Mel died how much it had shocked her. He'd gone suddenly, thank God, she thought now. He wouldn't have been able to handle a slow incapacitation. He'd died of a heart attack eating lunch while she was at work. She found him that evening stretched on the kitchen floor with a ham sandwich still grasped in his hand. When she found him, there was only disbelief. She walked out of the apartment door and back in, thinking she might be in the wrong unit. She did it three more times. Then it sank in. It was real. He was gone. And what a huge hole there was in her life. It was another loss that she'd never recovered from. Life seemed to be made of these.

There had been two men who'd raped her, and now there were two names. Yuki had never forgotten them. The older man was going bald, tiny dark eyes buried in a doughy face. He wheezed and reeked of cheap vodka. Larry Voyce. Yuki remembered his voice. He sounded like he chewed glass. A serpent tattoo wound around his right bicep. He worked in one of the two kitchens.

And the boy, probably only eighteen or nineteen at the time, which meant he was now in his late seventies. Devin Richter. The last time she'd seen Devin Richter he was playing ball with an all-white team against one of the Japanese teams. He was batting and he swung at the ball and missed. It was the last time she'd seen him.

She typed "Larry Voyce" into Google and came up with a smattering of results. Adding Idaho and Minidoka didn't help. She typed in, again adding qualifiers. Only Devin Richter pulled up anything of interest, a former minor league baseball player from Eden, Idaho with the same name. Reading the first entry, Yuki found out he had played ball with several teams in several leagues – The Billings Mustangs, the Idaho Falls Yankees, the Boise Braves – from 1947 through 1959, then disappeared. The next entry had a photo and mentioned some awards. The photo was of the man who had raped her.

He had aged, not in an unhandsome way. He had a rugged rangy look, pale hair that cowlicked easily. He rested a bat over his shoulder in a lazy, unconscious way that she'd seen him do many times at Minidoka. Coach Devin to the Japanese boys, and he'd been a good one, taking them outside the fence to a couple of championships. Another website mentioned his marriage to Agnes Crowley in Boise, and stated that they settled there. There was no photograph of the bride and groom.

She pulled up the national white pages on her computer and searched for Devin Richter in Boise, Idaho and came up with one hit. She stared at the number and it seemed to vibrate on the screen. She was scared to go on, but she forced herself to hit "Print."

May 9

YUKI AND HER FRIEND Karen Pope sat at a sidewalk café just off Pike Street Market in a skinny strip of sun. Yuki was drinking ice water with lemon and nursing a small Cobb salad, while Karen was halfway into an IPA and devouring a Reuben.

"Given what you're going through, I'm going to do whatever I want from now on," she'd stated dramatically to Yuki just after ordering. "Bring on the butter, booze, and unsafe sex. Cancer doesn't care if you deserve it, it just shows up, the rude boy of the party."

As Karen's grand-daughter Michelle had noted some time ago, Yuki and Karen had "day and night hair." Yuki's hair, now a wig, had been jet black, while Karen wore her snow-white hair clipped short, and her tanned skin set off beautiful silver earrings. She was a big woman, strong, and her smile explosive.

Yuki was shedding years of silence in a torrent of confessions that unfortunately still felt too much like confessions, telling her therapist, then David, and now Karen about the rape. Karen had done what Yuki was still unable to do since the therapist's office. Cry.

"God, I am so sorry, honey." She covered Yuki's

small hand with her own as tears rolled down her face. "I can't believe you've kept it buried this long. You never even told Mel!?"

"No. I thought it might hurt what we had. I had a friend once who told her husband she'd been raped and he…." She trembling, "and he began to hate her."

"Jesus, men!"

"I found him, one of them, anyway. He's still living in Idaho. I did a Google search and couldn't turn up the older one, but Devin Richter the ballplayer, I found."

"A ballplayer?"

"Baseball. He was a coach at the camp. He coached my brother."

"Bobby? He coached Bobby? And he raped you? And you never told a soul? Jesus Yuki, I am so fucking sorry."

Yuki couldn't answer. She felt her throat constrict, her heart skitter around her chest.

Karen held her hand, squeezed hard, held, and after a moment Yuki's face relaxed.

"So, you called him?"

"It took me a day to work up the courage."

"It must have been so hard."

"It was. I sat staring at the phone for what seemed hours."

"But you found him?"

"The first number turned out to be his son, Devin Jr. Devin Jr. told me his dad was in the Cottonwood Nursing Home in Twin Falls, Idaho suffering from advanced diabetes, Parkinson's, and heart trouble. He went downhill fast after his wife died. He can't walk, even with a walker. He gets around with a wheelchair."

"How old is he?"

"He's eighty."

"Whew."

"Devin Jr. could have talked all day. I told him I was an old friend of his dad's. It turns out the second number belonged to his uncle. It seems the family liked the name Devin."

"So, you talked with his dad? The guy? The coach?"

"I called the Cottonwood Nursing Home – his son gave me the number – and they said he was resting but I could call tomorrow."

"That's today! Are you going to?"

"Should I? Where am I going with this? What do I want to do?"

"If someone had raped me, and that bastard McCormick almost did, I'd cut off his cock with a Newberry castrating knife." Karen laughed brusquely. "But I'm just an old Montana ranch girl."

Yuki picked up her water and her arm quivered, then she set it back on the table.

"You okay?" Karen asked.

"What is okay?"

Karen held Yuki and brushed at her tears with a napkin.

"I'm sorry."

"Never be sorry. You've been sorry far too long." Karen's eyes were hard, then sun flowed through them.

"What does your counselor say about it?"

"No rights or wrongs. Follow my heart. That kind of stuff."

"I thought you liked him?"

"I do. He's good." She smiled wanly. "I just get so depressed sometimes. And I've been thinking a lot about why I want to contact him, Devin. What my motivation is, what I would do?"

"And?"

"I'm scared of what I want."

'Which is?"

"I want to look the man who raped me in the eyes and tell him the hell he made of my life. I want him to die knowing I found him."

May 10

DAVID OSHIRO'S VOICE BROKE through the intercom when Yuki pressed the button.

"Hi, love. I was worried about you. Can I come up?"

Relief flooded her as she buzzed him in. David was someone she couldn't go wrong with. He went way, way back. He was dressed in jeans and a lime linen blazer, and held a small painting wild with impatiens under his arm. Yuki was in her plum bathrobe and wigless.

"You shouldn't have dressed up for me." David laughed. His smile seemed wise and kind and brotherly. They hugged and David gave her a peck on the cheek, then handed her the painting.

"Here. It's an early one, but one of my favorites. I figured you could use all the color you could get."

"Oh, David, it's lovely. Thank you so much." She took the painting and leaned it against a couch pillow. "This is so beautiful."

"I saw these flowers in Hawaii at a place on Maui called the Blue Pool. You hike along the ocean for about a hundred miles, then there's this waterfall pouring from the cliffs into a gorgeous pool. Very deep and clear. And growing profusely from all the cliffs are these Fucking! Incredible! Impatiens! They looked so brilliant, wild, and exhilarated I had to give them to you."

"Thank you *so* much, David, you shouldn't have. You are such a special friend." Yuki burst into tears.

"Now, now." David took her and hugged her, and she rattled against his arms, finally, deliriously giving in and letting go. David never let go.

She came back to herself after a long, long time.

"Sorry, David. I think I blacked out."

"You did, but I had you."

"Thank you."

David just smiled at her.

"Where should I hang it?"

David released her, stared at her affectionately, then looked around thoughtfully. "Why not keep it there for a while? Against the pillow."

"On the couch?"

"Yeah. I think the flowers have been exhilarated for so long they could use some rest." The smile still played around the corners of his mouth.

"Oh David, you're a saint. Would you like some tea? Coffee?"

"A glass of water would be perfect. But I actually came to take you to the Arboretum."

"I don't think I can walk very far."

"I've got a wheelchair in the trunk."

"A wheelchair?"

She thought how much fun it would be for David to push her around the gardens, riding on a slow train through the azaleas, rhododendrons, cotoneasters on the serpentine paths, the emerald lawns.

"You don't like the idea? The wheelchair part? I could carry you on my back."

"I should hate you for this, David, but I love it! It's perfect!"

They'd stopped for a rest at the bench under a trellis of blooming wisteria, and the air was alive with the rich summery humming of bees. They were sitting quietly. David had his sketch pad out and was drawing a stone lantern with a fern behind it.

"I could get into this life, Yuki. Pushing you around in a wheelchair, sketching in the sun."

"Don't get too used to it, David. I won't be around much longer." She felt light, almost weightless, a rare joy. She took off her wig. "I like the feeling of not having hair. I've carried my long, heavy hair all my life. I never conceived of not having it."

"We all carry weight. Just look at me." He patted his rounded belly. "It's strange what one accepts as one's life."

"Or doesn't accept."

"Hmmm." David furrowed his brow and concentrated on rubbing a pencil on the pad.

A cumulus cloud crossed the sun and Yuki's face darkened.

"Do you think about it much, David? Being Japanese, here in another country?"

David grinned. "You want to talk about *heavy* stuff, eh?"

"Yeah," Yuki's smile was so soft it touched the air, "I guess I do."

"I don't think about it much, Yuki. There's enough of us here in Seattle to make it comfortable, and I hang a lot with artists who tend to be cool. And growing up in San Fran I was in Chinatown, and we had more hostilities with the Chinese than with the Americans. Where are you going with this?"

"I've been thinking about the rape a lot, David, and that's taken me back to Minidoka. I was a girl then, in a girl's world, and as kids we let our parents do the heavy lifting. Kids are kids wherever. We created games and played constantly, but there were always the watch towers, the armed military, and tall fences. The whole darkness, the tragedy of it is coming back. It's like a storm cloud on the horizon."

"Yuki, love, it's over. It was a long time ago. Look what our native country did. Look what Japan did in China, Nanjing. They weren't saints."

"It's not over yet, David." The sun caught her face and flushed it. "For me it's just beginning."

May 11

I am praying for strength to whatever deities haven't jettisoned me yet. There is vomit everywhere. Everything came up at once, and when there was no more, my stomach began breaking apart. And there is only one person to clean it up. Which I do, dropping the worst rags into the trash under the sink. If I could smell, it would be much worse. After I have the least soiled rags in the washer, I sit on the couch and smoke a cigarette, which I quit years ago, and stare at the card the Hospice Nurse gave me. She penciled in her cell number on the back.

I am so weak I can barely walk the ten feet to the bathroom and back to the bed. The carpet is damp, the air seems thick. I open the curtains, open the window. There are stars scattered between the branches of the fir out the window, stars all over the sky. I suddenly am greedy for stars. I want to cram as many of them into me as possible. It occurs to me that I might want to die.

Vomit on my blouse, and my right breast nearly hanging out, but I can't stay awake any longer. Leaving the curtains and window open I

*lie down and drift into sleep. Sleep is like water;
it washes me away. It's baptismal, and I dream
I have gone to a river with my sister and mother.
We are crouched on a sandbar that stretches into
the river like a finger; we are looking at tiny
shells. Freshwater mollusks wrapped in their
conical homes. And then I am laughing. There
is the music of wind, water, sun, the buzzing
green of lush foliage by the river.*

*When I wake up, I feel I have visited a far-
away land that is somehow also immediate. I
hunger to return. I write these words trying to eat
a piece of plain toast and drink a cup of tea.*

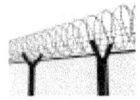

Alice managed to call at least once a day, squeezing
the calls into the cracks of her life, but still it was nice.
They'd had dinner one night, or rather Alice did. Yuki
sucked on ice cubes and sipped a 7-Up. Yuki told
Alice all about her visits to Raymond Sturgis, the
bereavement counselor, but stopped short of telling
her about the rape. Yuki felt embarrassed and
protective, and something else she couldn't yet
identify.

Alice had taken the advising role, and advised her
to sell her business and take a trip.

"Go somewhere you always wanted to explore.
The Great Wall of China, Macchu Pichu. Float the
Amazon."

"I don't have the energy for any of that, honey."
Yuki was smiling less at what Alice said, than her naïve

enthusiasm.

"How much energy can it take to float the Amazon, for God's sake? You just sit and watch jungle flow by, and people give you food and drink." Alice gestured theatrically with a fork. "If not the Amazon, then go to Hawaii and lie on a beach. That's what I'd do."

Yuki remembered going to Maui with Mel and Alice when Alice was around six. Alice had been tireless in chasing the waves out, shrieking as they chased her in. They had done some hiking around Haleakala and Hana. It had been a special time.

"Hawaii does sound nice," Yuki said, thinking of the warm breeze and the sound of waves, the scent of plumeria and pikoki. The sun. It was drizzling outside. Again.

May 12

WIND FLUNG RAIN INTO the west windows with a careless dominion and drove it through the trees into the ground. Yuki had slept poorly and was in great pain. She took an Oxycontin with her tea and tried to eat a fried egg, but succeeded only in getting down half a banana. Then she was sick, made more tea, and sat on the couch reading the morning *Times* which was blessedly still delivered to her door. She'd seen Bill briefly in the hall, wrapped in a dark burgundy plaid bathrobe. They exchanged a few words, and Bill set his newspaper back down and went back inside, forgetting it. He'd be back out looking for it in a few minutes. Poor man. Yuki decided she would invite him over for dinner tonight. It was the least she could do.

Yuki had taken a manila file folder and four sheets of paper over to the kitchen table. She could hear the rain hitting the window, the wind gusting louder then receding.

In her journal she began writing what she knew of Devin Richter.

> *Baseball player, minor leagues*
> *I remember the last time I saw him he was playing baseball at Minidoka. They were*

beginning to let us go that day and our family was in the first wave. I remember watching him swing at a ball and miss.

1.) Billings Mustangs (1947 – 1949)

2.) Idaho Falls Russets (1950 – 1953)

3.) Boise Braves (1954- 1960)

Married Agnes Crowley in 1946 (deceased?)

Lives in the Cottonwood Nursing Home in Twin Falls, Idaho

I've never wanted to go back to Idaho. Even when Mel wanted to fish the St. Joe River and wanted me to come along, I refused.

Son named Devin Jr. in Boise (I will call him again)

The Senior has advanced diabetes, Parkinson's (this makes him tremble?), heart problems (?), can't walk (heart problems must be severe?)

In a nursing home waiting to die! Just like me

Yuki stared into the mirror and watched her face fracture into a pastel impressionist painting. The fatigue of flesh. Pores, blotches, a wisp of hair – not exactly fitting back together. Yuki put her head to her hands and cried softly. She was coming apart. She stared harder. A woman sharpened into focus. Sickly, pale, bruised bags under her eyes, wrinkles that hadn't been there a week ago, flesh sagging from her thin bones. How could she go on? She reached for her make-up case, then she set it back down. This is who I am now, she thought. This is who I am.

May 12, Evening

WILLIAM CORBETT III SAT on Yuki's sofa and stared through a glass of brandy, lost in some irrevocable reverie, imagined or not. Yuki had placed a tray of chopped vegetables in front of him and munched on a carrot. She had not touched her brandy, which Bill had brought over, demanding fine crystal, and poured for her. The carrot tasted like wood but at least it wasn't making her sick, as everything else seemed to. She had her legs crossed under her, and the lighting, her wig, and her petite size made her appear almost as a child, which Bill, turning suddenly from the brandy, commented on.

"I don't mean this as an insult, but you look like a child again, Yuki."

"I wish I were a child again," Yuki said, laying the remaining carrot on the platter.

"You don't mean that," said Bill. "Look at all you'd have to go through again."

"I'm not a Buddhist, you know. Or a Christian. I don't believe that life is intended to be suffering."

"Well I don't either, my dear, which is why God invented alcohol, but that doesn't negate what happens to us." Bill raised his glass. "To flesh in all its frailty."

"And I don't believe in heaven or hell, or any kind of afterlife."

"Not reincarnation? I thought most people of Asian heritage believed in reincarnation."

"Oh, Bill, that's a stupid stereotype." She laughed, picked up the brandy, and sniffed it. It smelled vaguely of rubbing alcohol. "You find me attractive don't you. Even in my current state."

"You are a goddess."

Yuki laughed. She was enjoying the attention, the flirting. "I'm hardly a goddess, Bill. I'm an old woman dying of cancer."

"And I'm an old man losing my mind."

"I'm trying to learn to *cope*, Bill."

Yuki picked up a tsukemono and bit into it. It was crisp and salty. She could still taste salt. She could still feel crisp.

Bill finished his brandy and poured another, a rather large second.

"Do you ever think of sex, Bill? Of making love?"

"Well you know I can't get the damn… thing…up." He laughed heartily and took a swig of brandy. "Why, I once was a plucky thing too, just like a rooster, crowing his stuff."

Yuki was laughing with him, but the winds changed quickly in her body and mind, and she threw her head back over the sofa, and sighed. "What happens to us, Bill? So young one moment, so aged the next."

Bill raised his glass but said nothing.

"I watched, rather like a voyeur I'm afraid, these two university students, a girl and a boy, chasing each other on the grass in front of the apartment. They were so coltish, their energy so contagious. For a moment I got up and danced, and I felt in love. Then I caved." She laughed weakly.

"Who were you in love with, Yuki? Not me for heaven's sake?"

"Oh dear sweet Bill, no. The strange thing was that I didn't know then. It seemed so elusive. I wonder if…?

"Wonder if what, m'love?"

"Nothing. I wonder if someone or something or some part of myself is trying to teach me something? I'm finally realizing that I can learn and change."

"True." Bill tilted the glass and stared into the liquid. "Never too late."

"No, that's stupid. Of course we change. We can't stop it. We try. We try to freeze our lives at the good places. I wanted to stay with Mel, with my profession, this apartment, my health. I wanted to freeze it there, and just go on with my petty little ups and downs. But life doesn't work that way. It just keeps on roving. In Buddhism they say everything is transient, and that all pain comes from trying to grip what will inevitably change. That makes a lot of sense right now."

Bill's head had tipped back and he was beginning to snore lightly. Yuki rescued the snifter before it tipped too far and spilled brandy on his trousers. She stared at him, thinking how men still had this little boy in them that was never far away. She could see Bill as a child, marching around the house, erect, holding a sword. But then why only men? Didn't she still have her little girl nearby? The one who'd been capable of joy and trust? Her little Yuki, who thought the world a large playground until she was herded up with other Japanese, loaded into trains, and carted off to an internment camp in Idaho. Her early teen years created by some Other, some One she did not understand. And even then, she made a game of things. The adults carried the weight while the children chased each other around the tarpaper buildings or stole food off each other's trays. And then two men took that little girl away. No, that wasn't exactly right. They raped her and demonized her and she hid. And in some way, she'd been hiding since.

May 12, Night

YUKI WAS LYING ON a cold wooden floor listening to footfalls running away. They just kept running away and running away and not stopping. And suddenly she realized it was her heart beating, that she was in her own bed, drenched in sweat, alone. And she was scared. She picked up the phone, then put it back. What the fuck difference would anything make?

She had dreamt the entire episode, as clearly and literally as if it had just happened. She ripped the covers off and examined herself down there, expecting to find blood. She saw only her pale stomach, and the few coarse curls of her black hair that had stubbornly refused to turn gray or leave her body.

She'd been returning from her new friend Akemi's barrack. It was after dark and she was already late, a curfew still in effect, so she cut down an alley behind the barracks. The scent of rotting cabbage and urine was overpowering at times. The night, still and warm, the moon wide and bright. She felt good, actually, considering.

She heard the men as she stepped into the alley. Two prison guards arguing. They didn't see her at first, focused on the bag they were passing. Yuki froze against the alley wall, but it was too late. One of the men raised his arm and pointed at her.

"Hey! You come here. Come here now. You're out after curfew, little lady."

To this day Yuki regretted not running. She wanted to run, she was poised to run, but she was terrified of what would happen if she were caught. And she was terrified for her parents. So she froze, and tried to shrink herself out of existence.

The man who'd spoken, an older heavy-set man with short graying hair, began walking toward her. He had his hand out.

"Come on now. We're not going to hurt you. We just need to check who you are. You're out after curfew. We'll need to take you home. C'mon now."

Yuki began crying and she dropped to the ground. As the man approached, the scent of alcohol and male sweat was formidable. She opened her mouth to scream but a large hand clamped it shut. She felt herself lifted and carried. She heard the older man whisper harshly "If you scream, we'll kill you." Then another voice she recognized saying "This won't take long. You might even like it."

It was the other man, standing back, holding the bottle naked of its bag. Her brother's baseball coach. Mister Devin.

The heavy man set her down on the rough fir floor, almost gently. She felt her underpants pulled down, then the man crushed her to the floor and she couldn't breathe. Then she was torn apart, and she felt her soul leave her body and enter the night sky. Later, she remembered thinking she would die here. Then she went numb.

After they were finished, she heard their footsteps on the wooden floor as they walked away, leaving her like some discarded trash. It was the same footsteps she'd heard a few minutes earlier. Her pounding heart.

Her underpants were torn and bloody. She stripped them off in the far shadowy corner of the public shower. No one was there. She was crying silently, yet so hard she could barely see. She gasped for air. She felt like she was drowning. She cleaned herself with the coarse folded paper they used to dry their hands, then she balled up the underpants and jammed them into a pocket of the red plaid frock she was wearing.

When she entered the barrack, her father and her brother were playing a game, bent over a board. Neither looked up, though she remembered her father grunting. But her mother, tending pots on the stove, gave her a hard look.

"Where were you? You were out after curfew. That's dangerous," she scolded.

Yuki didn't answer, and ducked behind the cloth that separated the women's area from the men's and took off her frock. Blood had leaked from the underpants and stained the frock. There was also blood on the front of it. She put on her nightgown and slipped under the sheets, praying her mother would not come in. Yuki was shivering so violently, she worried the cot might shake and attract her mother. She closed her eyes but the images returned. She opened her eyes and stared at the ceiling, her hands gripping the thin blanket. She could still not feel her soul, and wondered if it would ever come back.

Later, when everyone was asleep, Yuki slipped outside, and used a shovel that was leaning against the barracks to bury the soiled clothes. For days she worried that her mother would ask her about the clothes, where they were, but her mother never mentioned them.

May 15

YUKI SQUATTED, GRIPPING THE cool porcelain sides of the toilet with both hands. Wracked by fever and nausea, she pulled the chrome handle again, and watched the bloody mucous and bile spin away, and clean, clear water fill the bowl. Gradually her grip on the toilet lessened. Rocking back and forth on her heels, she settled into a sense of balance. The spinning water calmed.

Everyone squatted or sat cross-legged when she first visited Japan in 1973. There were few benches in public stations and offices, and very few chairs. Everyone possessed such strong legs, flexible bodies, and near-perfect posture. And now she was honoring them with this traditional posture, which she had surely practiced when she was young, before the camp, before the American government tried to break the Japanese of their bad habits.

In the other room the phone was ringing, and she heard the message machine kick in: "I can't get to the phone right now, so please leave a message after the beep."

The doctor's voice was flat yet grating. He wanted her to come in for a series of tests. He had scheduled her first for Tuesday. He said she'd be at the hospital for a few days, so pack accordingly. There was no sound when he hung up, and Yuki wondered if perhaps he was still there, listening. She realized she had no idea what day it was. Weekends and weekdays had lost any meaning. She knew pain was meaning. Sensation that she was still alive. "All life is suffering." The line from the Buddhist prayer book returned to her. She thought of the giant Buddha statues in front of temples in Japan. All life is suffering. But not then. She remembered being joyous much of that trip, introducing Mel and Alice to a homeland she'd never before visited.

Yuki managed to stand, and with the help of a wooden cane Alice had brought by, moved herself within range of her pills and the water tap. She took two anti-nausea pills, then hobbled back into the living room and sank into the divan. She'd only dipped into work twice since she'd been home and the mail was piling up. Her assistant Francesca Tabor had taken on Yuki's load temporarily, but Yuki's illness had caused a dilemma.

Francesca and her husband Robert, also a realtor, wanted to buy Yuki's business, but Yuki had not been ready to sell. On the other hand, Francesca couldn't handle all the work indefinitely. She'd have to put someone else on. And then Yuki would be...what? The phrase 'dead weight' reverberated in her mind. Yuki liked Francesca, her enthusiasm and business sense. She liked her slight lisp, which combined with her swift wit, caused many to view her as intriguing. And Francesca loved the business, and respected what Yuki had built. She would be a fitting heir.

In a meeting yesterday, Francesca had told Yuki of her plans to bring Robert on board. They would merge the two businesses. Robert and Francesca were young, energetic, and in touch with trends. Her counselor Raymond had also suggested she let go of the business, and she had fought him on it. It was one of the last things she held on to, but now she regretted her outburst. She was hanging on to things that would be taken from her. Yuki decided to call Francesca and agree to the purchase.

May 23

YUKI CAUGHT THE PHONE on the third ring. She was moving from Playing the Lute to Repulse Monkey, having begun a morning Tai Chi ritual, something she'd done periodically over the course of her life. It was difficult, painful, and often she was so weak she had to quit before she'd gotten far, but it felt good to be moving, to return to this something that required discipline, that was concrete.

Karen Pope's sonorous voice rippled across the airwaves, or whatever waves they were, Yuki was unsure. Sometimes it felt like everything was made of waves and she was wind across them.

"Yuki. How are you?" Karen's voice sounded distant and hollow.

"I'm better, believe it or not. The doctor took me off chemo."

"Oh? How come?"

"He told me he'd put me on it not to cure me, which is apparently impossible at this stage, but for palliative reasons. But I told him it's making everything worse. The nausea was terrible."

"Well that's good then."

"Yes. I've been doing Tai Chi. I started it a week

ago," Yuki answered.

"Good for you, girl! I'll get serious about all that health stuff someday, but until then I'm going to continue taking lessons from my cat. Sleep a lot and feel no guilt."

Yuki listened to silence with patience. A minute, two, maybe three went by.

"Hey, I'm calling about a concert. The Fern Island String Quartet is playing a house concert in Magnolia and I have an extra ticket. The house is owned by a darling couple of retired weirdoes. You'd love them. The woman, Sharon, is old school Europe, and her partner, Desta, is a musician from Ethiopia. It will be very, very low key. Very. About twenty people. An hour and a half concert. You could come by for dinner beforehand. If you still eat."

Yuki's immediate reaction was to say no. She hadn't done any socializing in groups since she was released from Fircrest, and hadn't driven much. However, a plan was starting to coalesce in her mind, a plan that would involve both socializing and driving. A lot of driving.

"Yes, I still eat. Once in a while. It still comes up sometimes, but I've returned to the fine art of squatting. I had an egg for breakfast. Two radishes and rice yesterday."

"God, I want your diet!" Karen said, laughing. "Seriously, why don't you come by my place about 5:30. We'll eat here and drive over together." Karen lived on Capitol Hill. "Oh, I forgot, are you driving yet?"

"I haven't been much but this is a good excuse to practice. I might not be able to drive after dark, though. Could I stay with you if I can't make it home?"

"Of course, Yuki. I have the guestroom. Just pack your pills and a change of clothes. I'll see you around 5:30. Call me if you can't make it. Or even think you can't. I want to see you. I know I'm being selfish as hell, but I want to imagine it's like it was. When we did things together. Back before…all this…shit!"

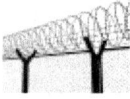

It was mild and misty when Yuki pulled out of the underground parking lot and turned right into the street. The windshield wiper blurred the trees, buildings and sky into an abstract, then cleared it. Driving felt strange to Yuki, as if she were playing a role. The car smelt of lilac air freshener, and for no reason she honked the horn, then again. She giggled. Then, as she was descending Queen Anne, Yuki felt the car get away from her, and for a split of a split second she almost let it go. Instead she slammed on the brakes and screeched to a halt in the middle of the street, which set off another fit of giggling.

She lucked out and found a place to park near Karen's apartment. With the help of the cane, she hobbled through the soggy yellow-lit night to Karen's rust-brick building. She thought everything too beautiful in night's light, and felt lightheaded in the ache of deep melancholy. She rang the bell and was buzzed in.

Karen opened the door and immediately hugged her.

"You're out in the world! This is wonderful. I started worrying after I invited you that you weren't ready for this; that you weren't up to it, that something might happen. God!" She hugged Yuki again, too hard, and didn't let go right away, then she did, almost with embarrassment, and stepped out of the way. "Come on in. Let me take your coat." Yuki handed over her lavender jacket. She felt the warmth of the familiar apartment and knew it smelled wonderful. The walls were a tasteful light rose, patch-worked with art. She watched Karen hang her coat in the hall closet, straightening it, brushing out the wrinkles.

"I've poached some sea bass, not the Chilean kind of course, which is endangered, but the Costa Rican variety, which is not. I'm getting so politically correct it sickens me." Karen belted a laugh. "I hope you can eat it."

"I'll try my best," Yuki said. "Do you know all the people at the concert?"

"Oh God no, silly, only a few. I do business with Sharon on a regular basis. She invites me to things. Have a seat. Would you like a glass of wine? They've got a good Chardonnay, a Semillion, a Viognier, what else, something else? Oh God, I'm nervous. Are you okay?"

Yuki laughed. "You have made me laugh. What a wonderful gift. A glass of water would be fine."

Karen returned with two glasses, handed the water to Yuki, and toasted her, clinking their glasses together. "To Yuki, who has been through far too much and needs a relaxing night off."

Karen sat, angled her chair. "So, how are you?"

She stared at Yuki maniacally. "Wow, feels great to get that off my chest."

Yuki looked around. It had been several months since she'd been in Karen's apartment. She liked the cluttered ease of it; the knitted blanket hanging off the loveseat, the piles of books and magazines, the photograph of some Nepalese or Tibetan mountain tipped a hair to the right. Karen taught literature at the University of Washington and had always given prime real estate to books.

"Oh, I'm okay as long as I don't think about it. Up and down. Some days I have no energy. The pain can be excruciating and I don't like to take pills, but that's what I do."

"Are you still going to the bereavement counselor?"

"Yes. Raymond's been a wonder. I have the feeling he wants me to do something crazy. Go out with a burst of flame."

Karen laughed. "Like Thelma and Louise?"

"I am thinking about a road trip."

"Really! Where?"

"I'm thinking about driving to Idaho."

"No!! You're not? You're not going to visit that man? Devin?"

"I'm thinking about it."

"You want company? I could take some time off."

"That would be too Thelma and Louise-y," Yuki said, laughing.

"I'm serious, Yuki. You might need a hand here and there."

"I won't be coming back."

"Oh, don't be silly. Think about it. I'd love to help out and keep you company."

Yuki took another sip of water and said nothing. This had been her life, the

socializing, wine, good food and good friends, concerts, movies. Now it seemed like a brittle shell that could shatter at any moment.

The sea bass tasted warm and salty, and the texture was flaky. The broccoli tasted similar but the texture was different. And the buttered rosemary bread was similar with yet a different texture. But she didn't want to disappoint Karen, so she sliced pieces and chewed and swallowed them, and told Karen how delicious it all was. As she drank her water, she remembered the fruity acrid taste of a good Chablis.

Yuki found her imagination traveling back to Minidoka. Her mother had crocheted a basket of fruit and hung it on the wall. The fruit was vivid, almost garish, but its hyper-reality was so distinct from the drabness of the landscape and camp, that it became symbolic of everything the camp was not. And now she was losing her taste, her smell, possibly soon other senses. It was as if she was being sent back to a place of drabness, blankness – imprisoned in the world at large. Soon her mobility would be gone as well.

Karen's chatter brought her to the surface, and the warmth of the apartment erased Yuki's sudden chill. Again, Yuki felt sudden hilarity, and began giggling madly.

"What?" Karen looked startled.

"It's just me," Yuki said, "returning from prison."

Karen watched Yuki carefully. Her giggling had diminished, and she looked lost.

After watching Yuki take her after dinner medication, six pills, and struggling to swallow them, Karen looked concerned. She asked Yuki if she still wanted to go to the concert.

"We could just hang out here and chat."

But Yuki insisted on going.

Karen drove, and helped Yuki up the steps into a gorgeous Queen Anne house whose living room overlooked Elliott Bay. A small stage had been set up in one corner of the room, and several semi-circles of folding chairs awaited what would manifest. Karen chose two of the folding chairs, and settled Yuki in one, then excused herself.

Yuki looked around, watching groups of people mingle and break apart. Karen was chatting with an older man and woman, and when they all began laughing, Yuki began crying softly. She thought she might never be happy again.

Then as the music started, two cellos and a viola playing a Chopin nocturne, Yuki felt the Oxycontin kick in and its artificial bliss engulf her, and she was happy she'd come.

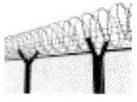

By the intermission the day had taken its toll, and Yuki asked that they leave. They returned to Karen's place, and Karen insisted Yuki stay with her. Yuki did not argue. While Yuki was in the bathroom, Karen pulled out the hide-a bed and turned down the sheets. Yuki sat down on the bed and told Karen she was going to

Hawaii within a few days. It came as a surprise to both of them.

"Can you manage it?"

"I think so. I'll take cabs. I shouldn't have to walk much. There are restaurants in most of the hotels."

"When did you decide this?"

"Just tonight. I need to get away. I need to put my feet in the water and get some sun. And I need to see if I can manage traveling." Yuki lifted the covers and crawled under. She'd taken her wig off, and it was the second time this evening Karen thought she looked like a child, this time a bald, gnomish child.

"Do you want a glass of water?"

But Yuki didn't answer, and for a moment Karen felt a surge of fear. Then she saw Yuki's chest rise, her heart slipping into the rhythm of sleep. Karen retrieved a heavy Hudson Bay blanket from her linen closet and spread it over her. This wasn't at all fair.

Part 2

May 25

YUKI FELT THE PLANE tip, and rising from a foggy dream, heard the flight attendant announce their descent into Honolulu. Yuki rubbed her eyes. She'd slept despite the vibration of engines, and the whining child behind her.

"Have a nice sleep?" The woman next to her with the kind face smiled. "You were out for some time."

"I didn't snore, did I?" For a moment Yuki was embarrassed.

"I've heard worse." She laughed.

Yuki remembered now the woman was going to visit her son who was a colonel in the Army.

"My husband," she'd said, "for one." She straightened her faux Panama hat. "He was killed in the war. The Japs killed him at Tarawa. And now my son's out here in the Pacific again." She said it simply, with no malice. Still Yuki was stung. What did the woman see when she looked at Yuki? A person? A Jap?

"Now my new husband doesn't snore at all. He wears one of those CPAP devices for sleep apnea. Just does away with snoring altogether."

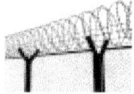

Yuki was instantly breathless and dizzy in the embry-
onic heat and humidity. She followed the passengers
to the baggage claim, passing lush elaborate gardens
below, palms, and red-leafed plants that looked like
fans. Her blue bag, sparsely packed, caught her off
guard when she tried to lift it from the conveyor belt
of the baggage return, and the man next to her helped
her, then walked her to a bench.

"Are you going to be okay?"

She nodded. What was okay? She sat, caught her
breath, and watched the vacationers in shorts and
aloha shirts, flip-flops and halter tops. Maybe this was
a mistake. She shook her head then looked up, around,
then stood. She was dizzy but fought through it, using
the wheeled bag as a crutch. Outside the airport she
asked an attendant to hail a taxi. She'd chosen a hotel
in Waikiki at random, graciously ignoring the
recommendations of well-intentioned friends. Friends
who thought she was both crazy or brave or both.

"The Queen Kapiolani Hotel," she told the cab
driver, a Filipino man around fifty with a neat pencil
mustache, "in Waikiki."

"You staying long, miss?" he asked as he lifted
her bag into the trunk. "Bag's a little light, eh? Maybe
some shopping? Bring some stuff back, eh?"

She wondered if she'd packed enough, then took
the cabbie's comment as an invitation. It had been
ages since she'd gone shopping. She settled herself in
the luxurious back seat. The windows were down and

the air smelled incredible. It was as she remembered. There had been a middle-aged Japanese man in Minidoka who looked like the cabbie. Mr. Haroto. He had given the children candy whenever he saw them, and Yuki still remembered the excitement and yelling of the children rushing to greet him and get their piece. It had earned Mr. Haroto the name "Candy Man."

The cabbie was friendly and peppered her with questions, some flirtatious, while telling her he was married with six children, two of them in school on the mainland. They were bogged in traffic, and the cabbie suddenly swerved and exited the freeway. Yuki stared out the window as they drove through an industrial area that turned seedy, then morphed into downtown Honolulu. The cabbie took a right turn, turned left onto Ala Moana Boulevard, and Yuki spotted the ocean, turquoise where it frothed the coral shore, deepening to cerulean, and turning midnight where it plunged. Oahu was an extinct volcano, and all the people gathered on the peak while the rest was underwater.

Yuki was suddenly exhilarated, giddy. She bit her lip to keep from giggling, and took a deep breath. The scent of tropical flowers, cooking oil, exhaust, and finally the sea, washed over her.

The taxi pulled up in front of the Queen Kapiolani Hotel, and the cabbie helped with her bag.

"You take care, eh? Be safe." Then he smiled and was off.

A bellboy dressed in a khaki uniform welcomed her and took her bag. Yuki followed, walking the low stairs slowly, holding the rail. The stairs were bordered by overhanging lava-rock walls, rife with ferns, impatiens, and flowers that rang out with delicious scents. Birds she didn't know flitted in and out of the open lobby, and as Yuki approached the desk, she saw pools of limpid water throughout the spacious lobby, spotted with lilies and koi. She was in paradise.

After checking into her room, 516, a studio with an ocean view – and fastidiously emptying her suitcase, placing her clothes in the ample drawers and closet, and her meds in a row by the sink, Yuki felt the buzzy excitement, the taste of magic, wearing off. Heavy and fatigued, she desired nothing more than to collapse on the large bed. But she fought it off.

She took out her one-piece jade swimsuit and put it on. It hid her incisions, but sagged on her thin frame. She slathered herself with sunscreen. She decided to go without her wig, and avoiding the mirror, she donned a floppy white hat, and took the elevator downstairs to the pool, stopping to drop her hat and towel on a deck chair.

The blues of the water were lovely, and she walked to the deep end and dove in. She had always been a gifted diver and swimmer, and the moves came instinctually to her. She did a slow crawl down the pool, under and a flip, then breaststroke back to the deep end. The water was cool enough to energize, and she did two more laps before getting out and walking back to the deck chair where she'd dropped her towel. In honor of Bill and Karen, she ordered a Mai Tai, lay back in the deck chair, and closed her eyes. Hawaiian music wafted from hidden speakers carrying Yuki off into the gentle air.

When she woke, the ice in the Mai Tai glass had melted. Even though she was now in the shadow of the hotel's wall, she could feel the sun on the front of her body. Yuki took a sip of the watery drink, got up, stretched and walked to the shallow end of the pool. She waded down the broad steps into the water until she was over her waist. It was cool, not cold, and felt ravishing on her burning skin. She dove softly forward and tried her awkward butterfly stroke to the far end of the pool. As she swam, she thought of the pond they'd swum in at Minidoka, where the incessant summer sun burned away anything in its path. She remembered the squishy black mud the boys would throw at each other, the tadpoles and leeches. So far away, yet immediate in her memory. She exited the pool, scooped up her clothes and the novel she'd brought down, and went back up to the room.

That night after picking at a dinner of a fish called Ono, rice salad and kimchi, which was the only thing she could taste, she threw up everything into the room toilet, and spent an hour sucking ice cubes on the lanai watching the waves froth on black water. Even though her chemo had ended, she had a difficult time retaining food, especially anything spicy or new.

It was after ten o'clock when she felt well enough to put on her sandals and walk down to the beach. The surf rentals were all closed, the catamarans pulled high onto the sand, and the lights of Waikiki, and the stars reflected, stretched, and shattered on the inky water. She took off her sandals and felt the sand on her feet, and it felt like heaven. She walked to where the waves sluiced around her and continued, stopping often, for a few hundred yards, past several hotels.

At one hotel restaurant a Hawaiian band played in the open-air bar, and Yuki stood and watched the seated tourists talk, eat, and gesture, while dark-skinned waiters and waitresses served them, and she walked on. All over the world, she thought, the dark-skinned people waiting on the light-skinned.

Another hundred yards, and the beach quieted. Here it was scattered with palms, and she sat carefully on the sand and stared out at the oily light on the black ocean. She felt in a dream. Every so often a person or couple, or once a rowdy group of Australians, swearing and laughing, walked by. To her left she heard the soft sounds of love, and looking over, saw the two bodies moving in shadow toward rapture. She remembered when she'd thought love completed one's alienation, made one whole; that she and Mel would lose their individual boundaries and form this new creature. And in a way she supposed they had, but now she was distinct, alone from anyone. One always returned to oneself. And then what? Did one return to something else? After?

She dozed on the beach, and was awoken by two policemen carrying batons. One asked if she was all right, the other suggested she return to her hotel, as they'd had some "incidents" on the beach at night lately.

As they walked away, she heard them talking. "Ho brah, fo' real? Bald wahines on da beach?" "At night, brah." "She don wanna be seen." "Wha you think?" Cancer?" "My Auntie Tika ..." Their voices faded.

May 26

In my dream I sat at a table in a bare room. There was only one chair, wood, straight-backed. On the table was a square box covered with barred rice paper. I knew that my life was in that box. I picked it up and shook it, and from within came the sound of laughing. I saw myself as a girl running through a field of wildflowers. They whipped my legs as I ran. I heard the sound of wailing. I saw myself standing in an empty warehouse. I wiped at the blood on my leg with my hand. I saw myself picking up my clothes and carefully putting them on. I heard the sound of wings, and suddenly, in the room there were so many birds. Their feathers brushed my skin and everywhere they touched it burned. I was setting the box back on the table when I woke.

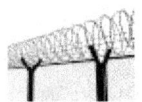

The next morning Yuki pulled back the heavy curtains, and sunlight flooded the room and dazzled her. She lined up her pill bottles like staunch soldiers in formation, and took them one-by-one with water. Her lower stomach throbbed. She hoped the Oxycontin would put some distance between her and the throb. She relied more on the contents of her little colored bottles now than the meager amounts of food she kept down. They had become her little warriors.

After dressing Yuki went downstairs and wandered through the breakfast buffet, amazed at the abundance of fruit – mango, starfruit, guava, midget bananas, papaya, pineapple, melon. She placed some melon, pineapple and a small, stout banana on her plate, found a table in the sun near the edge of the pool where a wall lava rock descended into it, and went back for a cup of tea. When she returned, a Caucasian woman with blond hair was sitting in a chair across from her.

"I hope you don't mind," the woman said apologetically. "All the other tables were full."

Yuki scanned the tables as if doubting her, but no, the woman was right. There were no other spots to sit. She was enjoying being alone, but nodded to the woman that it was okay.

"My name's Kathy. I'm here for a conference, but really just to play hooky and get some sun and water. It's still chilly in Montana."

"My name is Yuki," and as she was taught Yuki extended her hand for a light handshake. Kathy took her hand, held it, and let it go.

"Are you here for work or pleasure?"

Yuki thought about the choice and almost said 'Neither.'

"Pleasure, I guess. The weather is comforting."

"Isn't it? I love not wearing shoes! I hate shoes."

Kathy had an easy laugh, and Yuki felt herself relaxing as she nibbled on her plate of fruit.

"What conference are you attending?" Yuki asked.

"It's a religious conference. The overriding topic is Faith." She laughed at Yuki's startled expression. "I'm a professor of religious studies at the University of Montana, in Missoula."

"Faith is a curious thing," Kathy continued. "Everyone has faith in something. The sun will come up tomorrow. The plane that took off in Seattle will land in Honolulu. Without faith we couldn't live, we couldn't act."

"How does death fit in?"

"We have faith we'll die. Some people have faith that they'll be reborn and live forever."

"Do you?"

"In a way," Kathy said smiling, "in a way."

Yuki smiled as well, and thought this woman disarming. She felt a strange connection to her, as if she'd known her deeply in the past. Upon leaving, the woman handed Yuki her card.

"If you are ever in Missoula, Montana, look me up. I live alone, but I love company."

"I will," said Yuki, looking over the card, simple and elegantly embossed with silver. *Kathy Riordan, Professor of Religious Studies, University of Montana.* A phone and email. "I will."

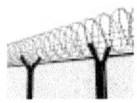

Later, in her suit and sandals, walking to the beach,

she passed a young man sitting in a small rectangle of grass, rock, and palm trees. The man's hair was brilliant orange, vibrant with sun. He sat slumped, holding crookedly a sign reading "HELP" scrawled on cardboard with a felt pen. Yuki could not see his face. The begging cup next to him held some change, a wad of gum, and a cigarette butt. He was surrounded by the shiny shops of Waikiki, their glistening windows like overly white American teeth. Yuki felt tears well up but walked on.

The beach was crowded and getting hot, and the sun on her bare scalp was a new sensation. Yuki couldn't believe how many Japanese tourists there were. She felt like she should know them in some integral way, but she couldn't even understand their language.

She found a small curved armature of sand that was partially deserted and settled on a blanket. Opening the book that had been on her shelf for years, *Foe* by J.M. Coetzee, she began to read. But soon she gave way to the weight of the sun. She closed the book and let her head settle on her arms.

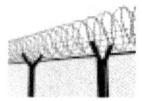

I dreamt I was walking determinedly across an arid, sage-covered plain toward a distant settlement. As I walked, I began to recognize the settlement as Minidoka Camp. It was the view I'd seen as I drove away on a clunky yellow bus, the day I left Minidoka forever. I struggled to

walk faster. I needed to reach the camp before it grew dark. I could see the sun falling toward the peaks in the west, falling toward night. I heard the sirens that called curfew, saw the floodlights snap on in the watchtowers, but I couldn't reach the camp. Still I walked, stumbled and went on.

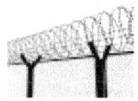

Yuki awoke with fever. She sat up too quickly and became dizzy, nauseous. She vomited her meager breakfast into the sand, hoping no one would notice. Her doctor had been insistent that she start drinking nutritional supplements.

"You'll absorb them quickly, before you vomit them out," her doctor had said, but she'd resisted. Now she was ready to try anything. She'd pick some up at the one of the small ABC stores scattered around Waikiki.

She breathed deeply, thinking about the dream. Why was she trying to get to the camp? Anyone in their right mind would be running away. Did this have something to do with what happened there? Her rape? Was the dream telling her she needed to go back to it? It felt like it was telling her this.

She made her way down the curl of sand to the clear water and walked in. It was baptismal. Her perceptions were so ragged lately, so raw. The world blistered. She let herself sink up to her neck, and as she pulled her legs up, felt the waters buoy and rock her in its cradle. Yuki began crying softly, her tears falling into their greater sister, the ocean. She was returning part of herself to the ocean.

As she walked back to the hotel, Yuki noticed the boy with orange hair she'd seen earlier. Now he was sprawled on the sidewalk, lying on his back. His mouth was open, but the only movement Yuki could see was his chest raising and falling very slowly. The boy's freckled face was angelic. A fallen angel in his late teens. People and cars rushed by ignoring him, the nervous energy of Waikiki unabated. Without thinking, Yuki walked over to him.

"Hey," she said loudly. "Hey, kid." There was no response. Yuki picked up his arm and felt a weak flutter of a pulse. He reeked of urine and vomit.

"Oh God," she intoned. She laid his arm back onto the grass then shook his shoulders. Several people watched her from a roof-top restaurant across Kalakaua. One of them, a young woman, yelled "He's been there all morning." She saw, rather than heard them laughing, then heard the word "dead" cross the traffic. She shook him harder.

"Kid. Kid, wake up. You need help."

He was dead weight and there was no chance of lifting him, but suddenly he coughed and began to struggle.

"Goway, goway." His voice was thick and raw.

"It's alright. I'm not going to hurt you."

The boy was on his knees now, breathing heavily. His eyes wild, like a rabid animal, and for a second Yuki was scared. But she held her ground.

"Whatyawant?"

"I'm going to help you."

"Donwannohelp." Then he belched, and a rivulet of blood joined the drool running out the corner of his mouth.

Yuki tried to prop him up, but he shook her off. She held him to steady herself. Then he stopped struggling and seemed drained of resistance. He seemed resigned to whatever destiny had in store for him. Destiny in this case was in the hands of a tiny, bald Japanese woman, not the cops. The cardboard sign slipped from his hand to the ground.

"Whermymoney?"

Yuki picked up the cup and shook it. "It's right here. No one took your money." There was probably no more than a dollar in the cup. "What's your name?"

"Terrence." It came out slurred, a blur of a name.

"Do you have friends here?"

He shook his head. "Shum guys."

"Do you have any stuff? Clothes? Possessions?"

Again, the boy shook his head. His hair looked like that of a clown, all copper springs.

"Let's try to walk. I'm going to take you to a doctor." Yuki had passed a walk-in clinic about a block back on Kalakaua.

The boy pushed himself to his feet, tottered, but did not fall. He seemed drugged but compliant. Yuki managed to get his arm around her shoulder at which point the small crowd at the restaurant across the street began to applaud. Yuki thought, "Why don't any of you assholes come over and help?"

She guided him down the street to the storefront that housed the walk-in clinic, twin snakes wrapped symmetrically around a winged pin on the window. Their reflection in the window was comical, a tiny bald Japanese woman, and an angelic boy with the hair of a clown.

The clinic offered a welcome blast of air-conditioning, and an old woman sitting in the corner looked up, as did the nurse at the Koa desk. Yuki sat Terrence in a chair and went up to the counter to register.

"Hi," she told the desk nurse, "I'd like to get some assistance for this young man."

"What is your relationship with the patient?" He'd immediately gone from a young man to a 'patient.'

"I suppose it's too much of a stretch to be his mother," Yuki said, smiling at the nurse. "So actually, I just found him outside, just down the street. I thought he was dying at first."

"He was actually in here yesterday, but he had no money so we didn't see him. I assume you're handling the finances this time?" She looked up at Yuki, arching her eyebrows.

"Yes. I can take care of whatever he needs."

"I doubt that," the nurse said, continuing to scribble information on a form. "Have a seat and we'll take a glance at him."

When Yuki came back, Terrence was shivering.

"Do you have any ID? Any money?"

Terrence attempted to get his hand into his pocket but his hand didn't seem to function properly. It looked broken, and she wondered if he'd been in a fight, or just beating on brick walls. The kid was a royal mess.

"Just sit tight. It will be a few minutes."

Terrence closed his eyes and let his head fall. He began snoring almost immediately. Yuki went back to the desk and asked for a blanket, which she received and laid over the boy.

There were two people ahead of them, but a skinny nervous man who sat fidgeting and staring hatefully at her and the boy, stood up suddenly and left. The elderly woman's name was called, and a few minutes later, so was Yuki's.

A different nurse, this one friendlier, helped her get Terrence, who was by now nearly dead weight, into one of the examining rooms, and wrestled him into a chair.

The nurse took his blood pressure and felt his pulse.

"Well he's alive anyway. Do you have any idea what he took?"

"None whatsoever."

The nurse asked Yuki several more questions she couldn't answer, then searched his pockets. The only thing she found was a used bus transfer.

"He's probably been robbed." She said it resignedly.

"How old do you figure he is?" Yuki asked.

"Seventeen, eighteen maybe. It's a shame what these kids do to themselves."

There was a tap on the door, and a wiry, silver-haired man in an Aloha shirt opened it immediately.

"Hi. I'm Doctor Earling. So, what do we have here?"

Yuki explained where she found him and what he looked like.

"Well that's awfully decent of you to bring him in, but all we can do is get him walking and send him back out there. Unless you're taking care of him, he'll end up like this again."

"You're making it sound futile."

"I've had some experience with this type, Ms...?"

"Waldron."

"Sorry to sound so cold, Ms. Waldron, but it's a tragedy. These young kids traveling here thinking they're going to paradise. Then they get stuck, run out of money, start using ice, or PCP, start doing robberies, make trouble for the police. They don't eat properly, they get sick, they take more drugs, they get beat up, robbed. We may have to ship this one..."

Yuki interrupted. "His name is Terrence."

"The nurse told me he had no ID."

"He told me his name. He talked to me before I brought him here."

"What else did he say?"

"To leave him alone."

"And you couldn't, could you." The doctor's scolding demeanor broke into a faint smile. "Well, as I was saying, we may have to send Terrence to Emergency and let the state pick up the tab."

"Temperature's below normal. 96.3," the nurse said.

Yuki watched Doctor Earling roll back the boy's eyelids and shine a light into his glaucous pupils. Then he turned to Yuki.

"You'll have to wait outside now." Another nurse was entering the room with a hospital gown and a washcloth.

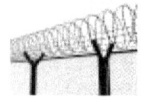

Yuki felt chilled from the air-conditioning and claustrophobic with hopelessness. She could not avoid her own life, which balanced on a precipice, and now she couldn't avoid the life of this kid.

"Do you have a piece of paper and pen I can borrow?" she asked the nurse at the desk. The nurse hunted around for a moment and handed her a pen and an index card.

Yuki printed clearly on the index card: *You have a gift I am losing, the gift of life. I am going to die soon of cancer. You are lucky. You could live a long time. Don't waste your opportunity. Go home and clean yourself up.* Yuki sat looking at what she'd written and felt suddenly foolish. The odds of this kid listening to her were remote at best.

"Could you make sure Terrence gets this?" Then she laid three crisp hundred dollar bills next to the index card. "This should cover any charges. If anything's left, give it to Terrence."

The woman gave Yuki a confounded look, and Yuki heard her saying, "Are you sure?" She left the office and walked into stunning sunlight reflecting off the many windows, and a blue, blue sky. It felt a little like hope.

May 26, evening

YUKI WALKED SLOWLY DOWN Kalakaua, resting on the occasional bench, watching the endless parade of tourists, hustlers, hookers, locals, and police slide past. The color and commotion had taken her beyond the realm of confusion and disorientation, to a place of strange calm where she watched everything with quiet objectivity. Every once in a while, someone would jostle her, letting her know she was still in the world.

Mid-block, a wiry Korean man thrust a glossy flyer into her hand for the Waikiki Shooting Range, an indoor, upstairs range just a few doors away. Without thinking, Yuki made her way to the elevator of the building's lobby, joining several military men and a group of four girls in bikinis and flip-flops who were flirting with them. In the elevator the conversation intensified, and Yuki felt a wave of claustrophobic nausea wash over her, then ebb.

The door opened, and she followed the group down a well-lit hallway and into a spacious lobby, where the petite blond girl behind the counter might have been selling ice cream. Instead posters displaying an array of weapons, everything from .22 pistols to machine guns, adorned the walls. She watched the group ahead of her point and discuss the virtues or various weapons, while the dull thud of shooting, interrupted by sharp rapid bursts, competed with loud seventies rock music.

When it was her turn, Yuki chose a 9mm Springfield pistol. The flyer offered her fifty shots for $25, as well as a choice of two other weapons, but the pistol would do. The girl outfitted her with a pair of ear protectors and called a male employee out on the intercom. The man led her into the range. There were thirty or so shooters, each with their own lane. Several men who looked like ex-military types wearing earmuffs circulated from shooter to shooter, answering questions, correcting technique, and offering advice.

"Have you shot a pistol before?" The man was a beefy Caucasian with a clipped military haircut. He had a warm smile.

"My husband took me shooting several times. He owned a handgun and felt that I needed to know how to use it. He traveled a lot."

The man looked at her solidly. "Did you ever have to?"

"No, thank God. I don't know if I could shoot someone."

"You could, if the reasons were right," the man said, leading her to an empty lane. "We'll start off at twelve feet, then if you're doing well, we can move the target back increments of ten feet. The clip has eight bullets. You'll have six clips."

Yuki nodded.

"Show me how you hold it."

Yuki extended both hands, bracing her right, which held the gun, with her left. She spread her feet three feet apart and sighted down the barrel.

"Good," the man said, "but I'm going to teach you something a little different. Pull your feet in a little so they're under your shoulders. There. Now bend your knees slightly and turn your support shoulder a hair, into the stance. There, perfect. You got it. That helps with recoil. Okay, now give it a try."

Yuki sighted at the bulls-eye and squeezed off a shot.

"Good," the man said. "You hit it. Wide about six inches but you hit the target. That's what counts. My name's Bill, by the way."

"I'm Yuki."

"Japanese, huh? I did some time in Okinawa."

Yuki fired again. High this time, but still on the paper. Exhilaration washed over her. It bordered on nausea.

"Say, you alright? You look a bit feverish."

"I have cancer. Not much time left." She fired again. Better.

"Well that's the shits. But they can do amazing things now days. My cousin recovered from cancer. I'm not sure what kind." He put his hands over Yuki's and squeezed. "Hold it tighter. Press in equally from each side." Then he stepped away. "I gotta circulate. Let me know when you want me to move the target back. Here's another clip. You know how to put it in?" He laid the clip next to her on the counter.

"No."

"Then signal me or one of the guys. And hey, good luck with that."

Yuki fired six more, then four with the new clip. Her arms were shaking from the exertion when she laid the gun down. In the restroom stall she was sick, but the feeling of exhilaration still clung. As she shakily made her way the three blocks back to her hotel the feeling slowly faded into the thrumming night.

May 28

YUKI STOOD OUTSIDE THE Seatac baggage return, waiting for Alice, chilled to the bone, knowing Alice, as usual, was just running late. Back from Hawaii, cold rain, and no daughter greeting her. She questioned why she'd gone. It certainly hadn't been an escape from life. Life just dragged itself along wherever you went. She thought about Terrence, the indifference he and others felt towards his life. What was this life anyway? An empty shell? A random genetic mistake? She sighed audibly. To most people, these kids like Terrence were numbers, cases, problems. Then for a flash her anger presided, her mercy turned cold, and she hated Terrence with every fiber of her being. She swore out loud, kicked at her suitcase.

Then as quickly as her anger blew in, her mood softened, "What a fool!" she muttered. "He knows not what he does." But then what had she done that mattered?

She couldn't stop the dark thoughts. They entered her like shadows. The sun and water and warmth in Hawaii enable me to go on, but to where? They are not preventing anything. Not even assuaging the pain in any real way. I am going to die soon. That is a fact.

I need to get real. I need to do what must be done.

Lately sleeping pills weren't working, and Yuki would wake up sweating and hearing wind roar across the Idaho plains. When she was at Minidoka, she'd been afraid of the sound of the wind, particularly in the winter when it was bitter dark. Her father used to make fun of her, telling her it was lions roaming, looking for stray children. Her mother would scold her father, and tell Yuki he was joking, but some tiny part of her was convinced. There were lions that roamed the camp in the winter dark. And now they were coming for her.

She'd ask her therapist for something to relieve anxiety. What the hell did one more pill matter at this point anyway? The Oxy and prednisone were lifesavers, dulling the pain, giving her occasional hope, and keeping her energy bouncing along. Yuki sat on her blue suitcase and surrendered to the chill. She watched three kids race ahead of their haggard parents and their off-balance mountain of wheeled luggage. Her one overnight bag seemed a contradiction to their life. Maybe the one who died with the most stuff did win. That made her laugh.

She closed her eyes, momentarily, and within seconds was back in Minidoka. She was back there so often anymore. She saw herself playing marbles with her sister and a friend, Mother and Father sat reading by the tin wood stove, all separated from the rain and night by tar paper and plywood. Life was like that, a veneer over death that waited outside.

A honk knocked her out of her memories. She stood stiffly. She felt suddenly so old, so sore. She watched Alice skillfully maneuver the BMW into a space between a cab and an SUV, yelling out the window as she parked, for Yuki to stay put. She'd get everything. And then she was being hugged.

"Mom! Welcome back. How was the trip?"

"Good," Yuki mouthed. Then she laughed. Alice could always amuse her, even when she wasn't trying to. Especially when she wasn't trying.

Alice hugged her a little too hard, a little too long, and Yuki felt her let go reluctantly. She's realized I'm leaving her, Yuki thought. This is going to be so difficult for her. Yuki's therapist said that people would hang on to her, not wanting her to let go. But that it wasn't their decision. She thought of Karen and her, in retrospect, almost desperate invitation to dinner and the house concert. Karen simply wanted it all to go back to the way it was. She felt her heart crack.

"Sorry I'm late. I've been working on this weird contract. Contract law is *so* not my thing." She hugged her again, then impulsively kissed her. "I missed you."

"I missed you too." She brushed a strand of hair off her daughter's forehead. "You got your hair cut again. It's too short."

"Oh Mom, long hair just isn't in these days. You got sun. It's mostly been raining here." She picked up Yuki's suitcase and walked around to the trunk.

Yuki got in the front seat, and a moment later Alice slid in next to her. Only then did she take her mother's hands and drink her in.

"You look frail, Mom. I thought you'd look more rested."

"I didn't sleep all that well. I don't remember traveling being this rough."

"Well maybe now that you're home you can just

rest for a few days. I can come over later and fix you some dinner."

"That would be nice." She smiled at Alice. "I don't even feel like I do anything. I'm tired as soon as I wake up. I take naps. I hate naps, remember? But most of the time I don't sleep. I just lie there and think or remember things."

"What things?"

"Memories. I'll tell you later."

Alice started to speak but cut herself off.

"You wouldn't let me take naps when I was little." Alice smiled ruefully. "I guess you knew how to shape a Type A personality."

As they drove, Alice filled Yuki in on a business crisis, an errant property that a Canadian living in Vancouver had purchased and defaulted on.

"Francesca can't find this guy anywhere, and he's six months remiss in payment."

"How much does he owe us?"

"Around $11,000 give or take. You need to call Francesca. I can't believe she didn't get in touch with you."

"I didn't tell anyone where I was staying."

"I thought you told me the Waikiki Inn. I called the number you left but there was never any answer. I couldn't even leave a message."

Yuki laughed at her mild deception. "Did you worry about me?"

"Of course, Mom, what if something had happened?"

"My favorite mantra. 'What if?'" Yuki lowered the window letting the chilled rain strike her face.

"What are you doing, Mom, it's freezing out."

"I'm throwing all the rest of my 'what ifs' out the window." She turned to Alice and smiled vividly, the hair of her wig blowing wildly.

"I'm worried about you, Mom," Alice repeated. "Sometimes I think you're losing your marbles."

"Marbles are the least of my worries," and laughing she peeled off her wig and stuck her head out the window. She could feel the heat from the heater on her lower body, while her bald scalp and face were stung by cold rain.

"Mom!! Mom. For God's sake pull your head in. You'll catch cold!"

Yuki finally pulled her head in, closed her eyes and sat back. The traffic ebbed and flowed. She realized that Alice was talking.

"…hoping you could help us out, Mom. We need to talk with someone knowledgeable. How about we have you over tomorrow night? We'll trade you a honey-glazed filet of Marlin for your expertise. I know you can't taste much, but you can imagine how good it tastes while you eat it. That might be close."

Yuki was suddenly disoriented and confused. She wondered if she'd already answered Alice's question; if there had been a question, and if so, what she'd said? Were the pills doing things to her mind? She remembered the store-front window of the walk-in clinic, her reflection with Terrence, the bamboo blinds pulled down. How we segregate disease from society, she thought, and wondered what would have happened if she had not interceded. Would it be any different now? Or had she simply nudged him a few steps further on his road to death?

"Mom?" Alice had turned nervously toward her.

"Are you good?"

They were skirting a Toyota dealership heading for I-5, the windshield wipers erasing the rain as it fell.

"I'm here, Alice. That's all I know for sure."

June 5

THERE WERE NO LONGER many stars, and Yuki's nights were long. Sometimes when she'd think of Alice, Yuki would begin to cry. When David came by, she held him and wouldn't let go. Chickadees, flocking in the flowering plum outside in the sun. She began taking pieces away: chickadees, the tree, the sun. Where do they go? Where will I go?

Some days there was such sadness, it pushed her back down in the bed. Other days it was pain, or stubborn lethargy. Yuki couldn't think her way out of it. Then Karen brought vegetable soup, got her propped up on the pillow, and spoon-fed her, talking all the time about this and that, the words sounding like a soothing river.

At the end of all this was a known entity, death, that was entirely unknown. People with their stories of heaven and hell, white light in tunnels, other dimensions, rebirth, enlightenment, nothingness. It could be anything. Yuki hoped it was like falling asleep, but losing even the small bits of consciousness she had while sleeping – uncomfortable positions, touching or holding her pillow, the fluid movement in and out of REM sleep. A total surrender.

Some days she wished it would come quickly, on others she wanted to fight, to never give up.

There was a small lunch at a woman named Cheryl's. Yuki had sold her a house once, and they'd kept in touch. The soup tasted good to Yuki, warmed her, and the conversation she couldn't always follow but it consoled her that people mattered. She remembered reaching for a glass of water, a buzzing intensity like angry bees filling her abdomen, and then it was later.

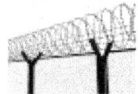

She was with her husband, Mel, and they'd just come out of a small square blue house, nearly the same blue as the sky had been. In the yard was a lone tree, but looking around Yuki could see that this was the last of a line of houses, all similar except for their color. This last house was adjacent to a patch of forest. She held Mel's hand, and they headed for the woods.

Initially they were very young, and began skipping across the yard. Yuki wore a long gingham dress that hung to her ankles. Her feet were bare. But when she turned to Mel, she saw he'd aged considerably. She knew he'd never make it to the woods. And then, with horrific clarity, Yuki knew she'd have to leave him and enter the forest alone. He'd fallen by now, and couldn't even gain his knees, and begged her to stay. But she turned and left him, ignoring his ascending cries. And as she entered the forest, torn by Mel's condition, his cries, but pulled by an irrepressible force, she saw Mel's face contort and become someone else, someone she recognized all too well – Devin, her rapist. He had aged as well, and was now haggard and bloated. She realized she'd have to leave everything she knew when she entered those woods, that there would be no turning back, no return. Yet she walked on.

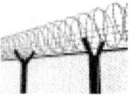

When Yuki awoke, she was propped up in a hospital bed and David was holding her hand.

"Hey there." David held a cluster of white calla lilies.

"What happened?" Yuki asked, her voice cracked, faint.

"You passed out at Cheryl's house. The doctors said you have a fever and that your white blood cell count is very low, probably due to your chemo. They've got you on antibiotics and have given you one blood transfusion."

Her right eye let go of a small tear.

"Why didn't I just go? Why can't it be over?"

"Do you want it to be over?"

Yuki sighed. "I don't know. I'm so tired." She closed her eyes hard then opened them. "I need to do something first." She squeezed David's hand and gave him a wan smile.

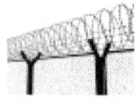

Over the next two days Yuki continued to respond to the IV and antibiotics. She was released into Alice's care Thursday afternoon, and Alice took her home.

"No argument, Mom, but I'm staying here tonight."

"Make me something grand for dinner." Yuki felt like a shriveled-up grape hanging on Alice's arm. A raisin, that's what I've become. She felt the vibrancy of blood flowing, nervous, sparking in Alice's younger body. I made her, Yuki thought, and now I'll lose her. She'll lose me.

That night Yuki dreamed she was lying down, and all she saw was pale blue sky. She could hear a distant roaring filled with voices, the voices of a river.

June 13

YUKI LOOKED THROUGH THE window at the wires behind her house looped from one utility pole to the next. They seemed again like barbed wire. It was becoming a common hallucination. She knew with certainty, that moment, that she needed to go back there, to Minidoka, Idaho; to her rapist; to live; to die. Living and dying were becoming confusing, intertwined. Perhaps dying is simply living with the awareness that one is dying. Or is that living?

She sat heavily in a kitchen chair. She didn't know if she was up to the task. She'd have to get rid of her things; say goodbyes, real goodbyes. Pack. She couldn't even think about it. She barely had enough energy any more to go to the bathroom. She had asked the doctor to increase her steroids, but he'd refused without seeing her again. Fat chance. She was through with doctors. They had given her a verdict she would have to live out, but she would do it on her own terms. Pain was becoming a real force. Her abdomen often felt ready to explode, and movement speared her. Her meds were becoming less effective dulling it. This is one reason people let go, Yuki thought, when the pain gets unbearable. Perhaps it's God's test, to see what we can bear. It seemed suddenly humorous, and Yuki began to laugh, which only caused more pain. Why would God do that? Cause someone more and more pain just to see what they could bear? What kind of test was that? She thought of Job, who she'd learned of when young. The lesson of taking whatever God threw at you without complaining.

The phone rang and it was Karen Pope wanting to go to a movie. "Or a play or dinner. I just want to see you."

"Karen, I've felt like hiding since I've been back. I have no energy."

"What if I bring you some wonderful cauliflower soup and talk at you."

As Yuki acquiesced, she wondered why her friends continued to ply her with food. The answer was reflected back at her as she turned from the phone, her reflection in the window painting her a gaunt refugee. That did it. Today she would pick up some of those tasteless supplements her doctors were always prodding her to drink. Ensure, or Boost. She'd tried one in Hawaii and gagged on the thick viscous stuff.

Karen arrived a half-hour later carrying a basket covered with red poplin.

"Soup and rolls. Homemade and heavenly. I used this amazing stilton cheese in the soup, along with gorgonzola."

Now that she couldn't taste much, it amazed Yuki how much of people's desire, their time and energy, were fueled by food.

Bill stuck his head in the door.

"A feast it looks to be."

"Come on in, Bill. You may as well help me eat some of this food. Everyone thinks I'm too skinny."

"As a rail, dear," said Karen.

"She's very sick you know," Bill said softly as an aside to Karen.

"I know," Karen said. She placed the basket on the table and went for dishes.

Bill pulled the cloth off the basket.

"Wine," he exclaimed. "Wine and women. We need song."

Yuki's doorbell rang for the second time that evening, and David Oshiro's voice erupted from the box.

"Sounds like a party," he said, giving Yuki a kiss on the cheek.

"You didn't bring any music, did you? asked Bill.

"I've got CDs in the car. I can run down and get some. It's mostly Brazilian jazz."

"That would be great," said Karen, handing him a glass of wine.

The evening evolved into an intimate affair, "complex with hints of oak" as David joked. There were times everyone was in tears, and others where they were doubled with laughter. And Yuki moved further down the road she was creating.

Karen had a friend named Adam, a gay man who was going to be a guest lecturer at the University of Washington for a quarter. "You don't have to get rid of a thing Yuki. He'll sublet it as is. It will be perfect. Adam loves flowers. He won't kill your orchids! You've never had this place as clean as he'll scrub it. He'll be here for at least three months, and if you come back early, he can move in with me for the duration. It's perfect."

"I won't be coming back."

"Don't say that, dear," Karen said, giving her a hug. There were tears in her eyes.

The phone rang. It was Alice. "Sounds like a party."

"I'm going away, honey."

"Where? You just got back from Hawaii."

"I want to see the camp again, at Minidoka. I want to visit Mom's grave. I've got to do it while I still can."

"Let me clear some time so I can come with you. You can't do this alone. You'll need help with driving, with the trip."

"I need to do it alone, Alice. It's the last thing I need to do, and I need to do it alone."

"What do you mean last thing? Don't do anything before I talk to you, okay Mom? Can we meet tomorrow?"

Yuki sat down and cradled the phone on her lap. She could hear Alice's voice yelling now, more and more hysterical. Everyone was staring at her. She snapped the phone closed and flashed an exaggerated smile, as if to say to her dear friends, "Everything is fine, everything is so not fine, my life is spinning from me.

As the friends disbanded, deep sorrow invaded her. All the things we take for granted, the multitudes of them, small acts, the placement of a hand on an arm. So many things. But never again for her, as short as her life might be, never again.

She tried to write in her journal that evening before bed, but her hand shook so violently that she just scratched the paper with black ink. It reminded her of a work in a German Expressionist show years ago called the "End of Writing." It was dedicated to a poet she'd never heard of and had never looked up, but remembered nonetheless. Paul Celan. After the horrors of the Holocaust, Celan claimed all words were false. Yet he tried to make them true again. And he gave them his life. And then she thought of that line of Samuel Beckett, whom she'd read off and on in college. Something like "I can't go on I must go on." It struck her as the truest thing she'd heard in a long time.

There was no longer any sense in denying or waylaying the inevitable.

When Yuki woke a few hours later, twilight was curling outside her windows, and as she lay there thinking about the trip she was determined to embark on, she began to strategize, something she'd always been good at. She'd have to break each day into sections, drive only an hour or two at a time, resting between. By her calculations it was almost 800 miles to the Minidoka Camp, and it would take her at least five days. She clenched her fist and beat it on the bed. She would do this. It was the last thing she would do, and she would do this.

Part 3

June 16

GIDDINESS ERUPTED AS YUKI drove downhill after crossing Snoqualmie Pass. She'd just streaked past two semis and glanced at the speedometer edging 85. An R&B station out of Seattle was buzzing in and out of reception. She pulled in front of the truck and slowed down, hitting the brakes too hard and causing the car to skid.

She'd topped Snoqualmie Pass ten minutes ago, and was amazed at how much snow remained in the Cascades. The last time she'd driven I-90 eastbound, she and Mel had driven to Montana to hike and visit her mother. Then they turned north and drove to Banff, where they spent four days, and then to Jasper, and after five days of exploring, had turned home.

Although that had seemed lifetimes ago, driving through the mountains brought Mel back, as if he were sitting next to her, pointing and naming peaks, discussing the complex geological features, talking about high-mountain lakes he'd hiked to, how the fishing had been, what he'd seen on the trails.

Yuki pulled into a rest area and was sick in the restroom. She walked back to the car, tilted the seat back, and closed her eyes. But her pain was so high-pitched that it ruptured her consciousness, fragmenting it, spinning it out of control. She was swept again into memory.

When she met Mel, she was two years into her own real estate business and he was a drop-out from the PhD program in Zoology at University of Washington. He spent most of his time hiking the Cascades and Olympics, and reading about Zen and Daoism. Yuki knew his initial interest in her was that she was Japanese. She remembered his disbelief when she professed to know virtually nothing about Buddhism. Worse even was that she attended a Lutheran church every Sunday with her mother. While Mel was trying to become Japanese, all Yuki wanted was to be American. Aside from her looks, and her occasional taste in food, there was little about her that resonated Japanese. She never spoke the language out loud anymore.

Mel had been trying to rent a cheap apartment, and had found a place on the north side of Queen Anne Hill, just above 15th. The house was for sale, however, and the landlady wanted someone living there to give it a homey feel until it sold. She needed someone who could move out at the drop of a hat.

Yuki was selling the house, and was arranging an open house when she first met Mel. She was attracted to his lanky carriage, the way he paced nervously, his husked voice, and the way his hands seemed to linger on whatever he touched. His lips were open slightly, as if perpetually breathless. When he spoke, he tightened words, carved them, and made them seem physical in the air.

"You're almost as dark as me and it's only late

June," she'd told him. It was the first time she heard him laugh.

"I'm outside a lot," he replied.

They spent that first night together in his rented house, for sale by Yuki, drinking cheap bourbon, and eating raw oysters and brown rice. He read her the poetry of Han Shan, Fu Shu, Wang Wei, Li Po and others. All people she'd never heard of, and because of that appreciated him more. He could teach her things.

"You're trying to seduce me by reading Chinese poets," she'd joked, and she smiled now as she thought of that. "That's not going to work," she'd said. But she knew she was wrong.

They'd lit candles and lay on an oval rug he'd bought at the Salvation Army. She remembered it smelled faintly of dog. And when he kissed her, she felt a sense of expansion that frightened her, as if she might lose control. Fear was a deep river in her, and control was what kept it within its banks. She'd left shortly after that.

But Mel was persistent. He had her card and called her the next day, and when she didn't return his calls, he sent flowers. That brought her back. Not the flowers, a selection of irises, ocean spray and delphinium, but his sacrifice. He had so little money, and had been so thin. Yuki didn't think she'd ever known anyone so thin. He lived largely on oatmeal, pancakes, fruit and some early precursor of trail mix.

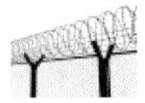

She stopped in Cle Elum for gas, and braced herself on the hot car until the dizziness passed. She went to the washroom, then sat on a picnic table across the road from the gas station, ate a banana and took her pills. She was chilled by the breeze, feverish from the high-country sun. She accepted most new sensations as normal these days. Pain had become a constant, the only difference was magnitude. The oxycontin barely dented it anymore.

The forest of firs covered the surrounding mountains with darkness, and she heard the ascending roar of trucks on the highway, then their quieting. She didn't know how long she'd sat, but the sun had arced, and suddenly a man walked a dog over, let it shit on the lawn, and walked away.

Yuki stopped for the night in Ellensburg. She was shivering after the last few miles. She'd nearly been run off the highway by a weaving pickup. Her hands shook as she wrote her name and address and license plate number on the motel register. Looking it over she couldn't read a word. The clerk, a pock-faced woman in her fifties glanced at it, frowned, and filed it away.

The room was knotty pine, and smelled of disinfectant. Yuki lay down on the bed and closed her eyes. Three hours later she woke. The TV buzzed, though she didn't remember turning it on. She walked out to her car. The sky was awash with stars and night shivered around her. The parking lot was deserted, and somewhere, not too far off, a dog barked, then barked again. She found what she was looking for on the backseat floor, a small red cooler, which she picked up and carried back to the motel room.

Inside were bananas, six cans of Ensure, a bag of almonds, and a chunk of cheddar cheese. She opened a can of Ensure and flipped through the channels of the TV.

She paused on a preacher who paced the stage nervously, his longish black hair repeatedly falling into his face. The power of the preacher's voice was startling. It soared from whisper to cry, a saxophonic crescendo of the word GOD he released repeatedly into the emptiness. The preacher had stripped off his coat and opened his shirt at the collar, leaving the tie dangling around his neck. He stabbed his finger at his audience.

"We are weak," he brayed, "and thus will inherit, for Christ said the weak will inherit the earth. So, we will be saved, but we should not haste to be proud." He buried his voice, turned away from the audience and stared looking up at the ceiling. When he turned back his eyes shone with fire.

"Because we are weak, we crave power; because we are weak, we abuse power; because we are weak, we believe our own lies! There is only one thing we can rely on, and that is God!" The man was roaring now. His eyes blazed white.

Yuki turned the TV off. She closed her eyes but couldn't erase the preacher's image. It burned in the darkness and radiated sparks. She remembered the older man who raped her, Larry Voyce, lowering himself on her, saying "Oh God" again and again until he finished. He had preached informally in the camp, a former missionary in Asia. He was, to many of the prisoners, a respected man.

Yuki drained the can of Ensure, took her pills

with tepid water, and lay down on the bed. She still saw trees flying by, felt the vibration of asphalt. She couldn't sleep. She got up and turned off the ceiling fan. Opening the room door, Yuki was greeted by unfamiliarity. An empty parking lot, and beyond, vast space stretching dark to darker mountains, the sky fractured with stars. Far off she heard a car engine roar, a voice yell, and then, nothing.

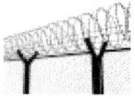

Yuki remembered standing in the night at Minidoka, alone, before the rape. She'd often get up after her parents and brother were asleep and go outside. She'd walk the long, lit street to its end, then turn right and walk a faint path, pulling back a section of fence that was loose, and she'd escape, temporarily, into the high desert behind the camp. When there was a moon everything glowed eerily but it didn't scare her. What scared her were the confines of her room, the domestic sounds of snoring and deep breathing. They seemed so transitory, so fragile. When she'd listened to her father snore at night, she realized now she'd been waiting for it to stop, his breathing to cease. In the vastness outside her Minidoka room, coyotes yipped and howled, far-off owls called. She heard the water rumbling through the Big Ditch, heard winds swish the cottonwoods. These gave her strength.

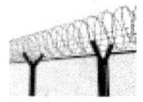

Yuki was suddenly very scared.

"What am I doing?" she thought. "What if I find this man? What then?" She began to sob until her frail body swayed dizzily in the deserted parking lot.

"I am truly all alone," yet when she heard a coyote howl, she knew she had the strength, as she had those nights at Minidoka, after the rape. "I can do this." She said it out loud to the empty night where God was hiding.

June 17

YUKI AWOKE RESTED AND oddly energetic. She showered, packed, and drove to a café on Main Street for breakfast. The décor was rustic, photographs of cowboys adorning the log wall above her table. She ordered tea, two soft-boiled eggs, and cantaloupe. She ate everything without feeling nauseous, and left the waitress, a veteran with peroxide hair, a generous tip. She was rewarded with a "Thanks, dawling."

The road seemed open this morning and traffic was sparse. She drove the long curves downhill into the Columbia Gorge, crossed the wide Columbia River, then ascended the other side. The sky seemed vast compared to Seattle, and the few clouds looked restful and relaxed. The landscape changed to farmland, then to ponderosa forest outside of Spokane. It was only 1:30 but traffic was already thick, and Yuki had reserved a room at the elegant downtown Davenport Hotel. She'd stayed at the hotel several times with Mel, and once with Alice. It held good memories.

After checking in, Yuki poured herself an ice water and spent a few minutes wandering the lobby. The hotel had been rebuilt since she'd been here last, and the new owners had re-emphasized the European magnificence the Davenport originally aspired to. Above the magnanimous brick fireplace was a painting of a clipper ship, its sails bulging with wind. It spoke of exploration, confidence, progress. Marble columns and plinths adorned the room, and vases over eight feet high stood like blushing symmetrical sentinels. Yuki peeked into a ballroom, gasping at the size of the chandelier, which was larger than her Queen Anne living room. Sunlight from a side window cut into the crystals, which sent it dancing around the room. She took several waltz steps across the room, then felt dizzy and stopped. As if a switch had been flicked, the grandeur was suddenly oppressive. It had been foolish to come here. This whole trip was foolish. She sank to the floor and began to cry.

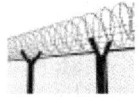

When she'd recovered enough, Yuki retrieved her luggage from the car and took the elevator to the seventh floor, then turned right and followed the hall to room 714. She inserted the key the wrong way, then reversed it and opened the door.

In the short time since she'd left the ballroom downstairs, a headache had seized her like a giant hand crushing her skull. She took an Oxycontin, then washed her face in cold water and lay down on the oversized bed. The road ran on behind the closed lids of her eyes, and she followed it until it slipped away. She dreamed that she'd walked out of the Minidoka Camp towards a distant ridge of mountains. She was barefoot and wore a simple cotton dress. As she walked, she couldn't help think the mountains were a mirage, that it was a trick of light that caused the horizon to rise into the sky. But she kept walking because even a mirage was better than the camp. And then she was walking through scenes, staged like sets at a theater.

At first these scenes were, or seemed random, but gradually they began to cohere, and Yuki sensed meaning. In several of the scenes she was running toward, or away, from someone who remained shrouded, indistinct. In several others, she was letting go of things – railings, hands, the steering wheel of a car. And in the scene that finally woke her, she was standing on a cliff overlooking a large river that flowed far below. She felt her fear dissolve as she took a step out into space.

When she opened her eyes, the room was bathed in a gathering of soft golden evening light. She had lost her sense of time, and for a moment wondered if it were morning. She got up carefully, her lower abdomen feeling like it was going to explode. There was a full-length mirror on the bathroom door, and after turning on the bath, Yuki stripped off her clothes and faced herself. She was bald, her wig on the bed. The crimson scar of her operation bulged like an evil grin, that of a serpent, and under it, her belly caved in. There was a spider web of red lines and dots on her chest, and her nipples seemed huge on her desiccated breasts. Her ribs stuck out like keys on a pale piano. Only her eyes blazed, luminous. Here was the offering of her body — fragile, pathetic and holy.

"Don't take me yet, God." She watched her lips

move as she spoke. They seemed to belong to a stranger.

After her bath Yuki decided that she couldn't stay any longer. Life was no longer this soft nor opulent. She didn't deserve this hotel, this luxury. She gathered her things and made her way to the hotel garage. Only after leaving Spokane and the valley and crossing into Idaho, was she convinced she was on the right path. The night was upon her, and the lights of advancing cars blinded her. She pulled into a rest area by Post Falls, let her seat fall back, and instantly fell asleep.

June 18

The days are like a ticking clock waiting for silence.

What is death like? I dreamt last night of barren rocks, bone trees, their flesh blown away. And incessant wind, a tangle of all the words I've ever said and ever dreamt of saying. I'm surrounded by my lies, my promises, my questions. But the wind is not enough. I long for rain, water. To cleanse me. To cleanse me of my wounds.

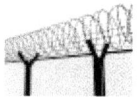

A harsh rapping on the car window woke her, and in the mercury light she saw the patrolman return his baton to his belt. A rush of giddy fear and adrenaline surged through her. She was instantly a little girl facing a camp guard.

Yuki straightened the seat and opened the window. The night air was cool. She took a deep breath to calm her shaking.

"You can't sleep here, lady. I'm sorry, but you'll have to move on. I gave you an extra couple of hours as it was." No apology for scaring her.

"Thank you," she said, instantly hating herself for being subordinate. Pain once more invaded her body. She wiped her face and noticed something crusted at the corner of her mouth. She picked up a half-empty water bottle, took a long drink, then started the car.

Yuki's fear subsided and she felt oddly calm as she drove through the Idaho night. The car clock read 2:53 a.m., and there was little traffic on the road except for a few trucks. Other than scattered houses the forest to either side was dark, and Yuki felt like she was driving through a tunnel defined by her headlights. She laughed at the idea. The tunnel of light. Would her life end in a cliché?

She struggled to find a comfortable position, finally setting the cruise control and letting her legs relax under her. She found a country western station that was playing melodies she liked, and when that faded out, some Mozart drifted in and out until she was over the Lookout Pass, but eventually she turned the radio off. Alone with the night and the hum of the engine and hiss of the road under her tires, Yuki felt a sense of peace, a resting place in her pain.

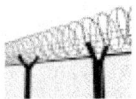

Hesitant rose was beginning to blush the sky when she pulled off the interstate near Haugen, Montana. Turning left off the exit ramp, Yuki drove under the freeway and past a scattering of dark buildings. Here, the road turned gravel and began paralleling a small wild river. She drove a little over a mile, bouncing over potholes, and the road dipped and crossed a wooden bridge. There was a one-car campsite with a rough-hewn picnic table. Yuki parked and got out of the car. She felt like she was vibrating. There was just enough chill that she could see her breath, and she pulled a wool hat over her bald head. She stretched, then pulled a down coat from the back seat and put it on, then the Styrofoam cooler and struggled with it to the table. Opening it, she found the ice nearly melted. Back at the car, the shopping bag on the back seat yielded a box of Grape Nuts. She retrieved a bowl and spoon out of her dish box, and poured cereal into the bowl. From the cooler she fished a carton of half-and-half out of frigid water and poured it over the cereal. It looked gross, and Yuki poked around in it with her spoon. Beyond her the river crashed against a large downed cedar and veered wildly to the left. The water was boisterous with spring melt, and stained with tannin from the mountains it drained.

Yuki was picking a raisin from the soggy flakes when she spotted the young man walking toward her, the top of an overstuffed backpack towering over his head. When he came close enough, she heard him singing.

The man, Yuki placed him in his mid-twenties, walked up to the table, turned, braced the pack on the edge, shook it off and swung it to the ground, huffing as he did. He gave a slight bow.

"Hi," he said, straightening and grinned, putting Yuki immediately at ease.

"That looks heavy," she said, smiling.

"Heavy is a state of mind," he said, smiling back. His thick blond hair was roughly cut and he sported weeks of beard. Despite the morning chill, he wore only a ragged pair of Levi cutoffs, a thick flannel shirt, wool socks, and hiking boots. The scent of wood smoke was heavy on his shirt. He dug a small brass stove out of his pack, and after scrambling over the bank for water, he lit the stove and placed a pan of water carefully on the flame. Yuki noticed he put out two cups.

The boy, as she now thought of him, withdrew a plastic bag from a muslin sack, fished into it, and dropped a few pinches of black tea into each. Soon the water began boiling and the boy poured water into the cups.

They watched the water steam into the cool air without speaking. The sun was close to breaking the rim of the stark shadowed mountains behind them. Yuki felt as if a great wave had dropped her here, a tiny bald grain of sand.

"Here," the boy said, handing Yuki the cup. He took the other and placed his bushy lips on the rim, sucking noisily.

"Genuine Keemun tea," he said after some time had passed. "My friend gave it to me when I left. They sell this stuff by the gram, like hash."

Yuki sipped. The rich, smoky taste so complemented the chilled air, the scent of pine, and rush of water that all she could think was "Perfect."

She didn't realize she'd said it out loud until he echoed it back at her and smiled. Just then the sun broke over the rim and bathed them in gold.

"Would you like some cereal?"

"Love some."

"Do you carry all your food in the pack? It looks

big enough to carry a horse."

"Got a ton of granola, and I forage a lot. I've become proficient at catching trout and killing grouse with rocks. I eat plants and some fungi. Haven't been sick yet, but I've lost a lot of weight. I was pretty heavy when I headed out."

"When was that?"

"I landed at the train station at West Glacier three weeks back. I've been walking ever since."

"How do you know which mushrooms are safe?"

"I've got a book in my pack that does a pretty good job. I don't eat anything that's questionable."

Yuki remembered when Mel became infatuated with mycology. She also remembered a couple of trips to the emergency room due to "mistakes."

"What's your name?"

"I go by the name Ransaker now. It means *seeker* in Norwegian, which is my heritage." He beat his chest with a fist in mock salute. "You can call me Ran. My friends do, and it's easier."

"Well you look hungry, Ran."

"And you look like Sinead O'Conner doing Yoko Ono. What happened to your hair?"

"It fell out." Yuki smiled. "When's the last time you ate?"

"Last night I almost ate, but the grouse got away." He laughed and his face creased delightfully. Yuki had always loved dimples.

"Really? Must have been a smart grouse." Yuki laughed.

"Hey, I'm a good aim. Only took me twenty throws to scare it."

Yuki busied herself getting a bowl of cereal, then

handing it to Ran.

"Here, put some of these in it." He handed her a bag of squashed thimbleberries. "And take some for yourself."

"Well thank you. You're quite the provider."

"It's been an interesting trip." He spoke between bites. "I've learned so much." He spread his arms wide, spoon in one hand. "Incredible. So much snow in the mountains. It's a white country. White and silent. It taught me humility." Broad-shouldered and weather-burnt, the boy sat on the bench and rocked back and forth, burning with nervous energy, shoveling cereal into his mouth. Here his similarity to Mel ended. Mel possessed an unshakable contagious calm. Yuki remembered one time when he sat so still at a picnic table by Darrington, that chickadees perched on his arms and hands while he told them stories. This boy seemed in continual motion.

She watched the boy spoon flakes and mushy thimbleberries into his mouth. He ate so raucously some of it missed and clung to his whiskers.

"How is it?" Yuki was smiling broadly. Ran's lust for life was contagious.

"Fantastic."

"Where are you going?" Yuki asked. She grimaced as she stood and something inside her twisted. Ran was staring intently at his bowl.

"As cliché as it sounds, I'm on a spiritual quest." He crunched mightily then stared directly into her eyes. "I get to these metaphorical crossroads — should I go up or down, upstream or downstream, walk at night or during the day, and I stay there until I get a sign. Sometimes it's just a feeling, sometimes it's a bird flying a certain direction, or a shadow moving a weird way. One morning it was a key formed by clouds. All day I looked for the lock that key opened, and I found it. Inside me. Something just clicked into place." He lowered his head and crunched again. "You see, there's ample wisdom everywhere if you know how to see it. Some would say it's God, but the Christians have ruined that word for me. I just call it wisdom. You just have to open yourself to it and it's there. The problem is we've been filled with so much shit since the day we were born, that it takes a great deal of emptying, and I do that best when I'm alone and in the woods." He looked up again. "Do you ever get into the woods alone?"

"Not since before my husband died." Yuki thought how when Mel left her in camp while he fished, she'd get really nervous. She'd channel the nervous energy into endless cleaning and rearranging of the camp. Sounds startled her, and peripheral movements played endless tricks and kept her on edge. She was always so relieved when Mel returned. She never admitted her fear, suddenly realizing that she had been uncomfortable admitting fear of any kind.

"Well, come on. Leave your car behind. We'll cross the freeway and head into Idaho. I've got enough gear, and I'm getting the hang of this food thing. And I'll give you plenty of space for solitude."

Yuki laughed. This kid Ran was so naïve, so crazy. Something she'd never allowed herself to be. Mel was far more balanced, patterning himself on the East-Coast transcendentalists like Emerson and Thoreau, a fellow who lived a mile from his mother. Mel would call Ran immature and impractical. But who could not be moved by his enthusiasm?

"I appreciate the offer but I don't think so" Yuki laughed. "But you go ahead if you want. I'm sure there's a lot more to be discovered."

Ran tipped the remaining cereal into his mouth and chewed, talking through the flakes. "You think I'm kidding? People have done it. Everett Ruess, Christopher McCandless."

Yuki remembered when Christopher McCandless was found dead in an abandoned bus by McKinley Park, Alaska. His parents were living in Vancouver and it was big news for a few days.

"I don't think Christopher found much happiness."

"Happiness! That's American bullshit. It's not happiness that matters, it's truth! Even the Buddha had it wrong. His path was to escape suffering, while the Christians revel in suffering. Everyone is so fucked up! At least McCandless faced death. Stared it in the eyes as it stared into the bus window at him."

"A lot of people face death." She grabbed Ran with her gaze and he stopped rocking. "Nursing homes are full of them."

Ran gave a shocked guffaw. "Well, aren't you a downer." Then he began laughing, rocking with it, and soon both of them were shaking with laughter. Yuki felt sadness, and its tethered anger, lift from her. This kid was good medicine.

It took a few minutes before either of them could talk.

"Now isn't that better than suffering?" Ran asked.

"Infinitely so."

"That's what life should be. One great laugh."

Yuki brushed a leaf off her pants.

"But don't you feel guilty? There is legitimate pain in the world."

"I'm trying not to do that anymore. Feel guilty. I was raised Catholic. Had a Jewish girlfriend. We were both cursed with it. We couldn't enjoy pleasure together. We were too guilty!" He laughed.

"Hmmm. Too guilty for pleasure." She wondered how much her own shame and guilt had affected her ability to experience pleasure. Yuki reached down for a stalk of grass and began chewing on it. It tasted sweet and fresh. Maybe her taste was coming back. "I think we all try and do what we can. If you feel like you're doing what you need to do, then I'm sure that's enough."

"I'll take that tacit support." Ran chuckled.

"You want me to feel guilty? Is that it?" She realized she was flirting with him, that it made her feel young.

"That's not exactly what I meant." Ran seemed a bit flustered.

Ran stood up, stretched and scratched his scalp.

"I should be going," said Yuki.

"Where are *you* going? I blabbered all about me. Sorry."

"I'm driving to Flathead Lake to visit my mother's grave."

"Wow. That seems brave." He smiled sheepishly. "I don't know what caused me to say that. I talk to myself a lot. Sometimes I say the craziest things."

Yuki nodded slightly.

"Where are you going after that?"

"Missoula."

Ran scratched his beard.

"What if I make you an offer?"

"What's that?"

"How about you let me drive you up to see your mom, buy me a good meal, then I'll drive you to Missoula. I have some friends there I want to see."

"Wow. That's a pretty attractive offer. I get tired easily."

"Okay then, shall we call it a deal?"

"How long do you think it would take?"

"If we left now, we could be in Missoula by evening. Early evening."

"What about the rule against letting strange men into my car." She was flirting again.

"I say to hell with most rules." He was smiling widely.

"This seems a good time to say that. But I see you didn't contradict my claim. That you're strange."

Ran nodded. "What good would that do?" He gestured expansively. "The evidence is pervasive." He stood rocking back and forth. Then abruptly said he needed to be alone for a few minutes. Without looking at Yuki for affirmation he walked over to the riprap bank overlooking the river and sat down.

Yuki began cleaning up, putting groceries back in the car. She walked into the forest to pee, and as she squatted, she felt presence above her. She looked up, and a pine marten was on a fir limb staring at her. Her legs were shaky from crouching, but she didn't want to stand and scare the animal.

Finally, she could take it no more and stood, tucking her shirt over her scar into her pants. When she looked up the marten was gone, but she was left with the immensity of its eyes. Like amber holes into something she would never know.

Ran was sitting where she'd left him, but stood up as she approached the car.

"Will you pray with me for the coming journey?" he asked.

"What did you have in mind?" Yuki laughed. "Five Hail Marys and a couple of Our Fathers?"

"Here." He sat down again on the berm of rip-rap above the river. "Sit."

Yuki scrunched down next to him, groaning hard as she settled.

"Does that hurt?"

"Most things hurt."

"Here. Take my hands." He held his hands out, palms up.

She placed her hands in his. They felt like tiny resting birds.

"Oh Wisdom of the Universe please guide this lady Yuki and myself as we journey on through your lands. Continue to give us signs that where we are going, what we are doing are the right choices. Make us aware and loving, kind, and open to your wisdom."

Yuki initially had to bite her tongue to stop from laughing, but she was touched by his innocence. He spoke so nakedly from his heart. He wanted to believe that he was on some mythic journey and would encounter his dragon, and that he would slay it. That there was something heroic in ordinary life. It was his time of life to have these beliefs, before jobs and families and responsibilities clogged life and its possibilities. And then she thought to herself, maybe my dragon is waiting in a wheelchair in Idaho.

"Wait a minute, I want to sacrifice something." Yuki got up as Ran watched her curiously. She walked over to the car and got her purse, dumping the contents on the picnic table. There wasn't much other than a wallet, a scarf, lipstick and her bottles of pills. She scooped the pills up from the table and carried them over to where Ran sat on the rip-rap, then with one smooth arc she heaved them into the riffle below, where the river slammed the huge granite slabs. They bobbed gaily in their fluorescent orange and green bottles until they were out of sight. Ran started to speak but stopped. For a few minutes after the bottles were gone neither of them said a thing. Then Yuki spoke.

"Okay, take me to Flathead and I'll buy you a meal. Come on before I change my mind."

Yuki popped the trunk while Ran maneuvered and crammed the pack in, then settled in the passenger's seat. As soon as she got in, she smelled his strong sweat mixed with wood smoke, and damp, and forest.

"It's a beautiful day." Ran was smiling and tapping on the dashboard.

Yuki laughed. "There used to be a band called that. They played really nice songs."

"Never heard of them, but it's a great name. Beauty is all we have, but we have to be so alert for false beauty. It's of the Devil's making."

"I thought you didn't believe in God or the Devil."

"No, no, not exactly. I said I didn't like the word God." Ran rocked back and forth in his seat. So much energy it had to escape his body. "It's too limiting. Consider all the people who think God is some old man who looks like them sitting in a throne up above them. Well their first mistake is that up is entirely relative. It's really out, not up. And out into what?! Some vast morass of universe within universe that's rushing across space or time or both faster than we can imagine? And why does God have to look like man? Simply because the Bible said 'He made us in His image?' There's a lot of shit in the Bible. There's even a lot of different Bibles." He chuckled, but Yuki sensed an edginess.

"And the Devil?" Yuki asked as he turned hard onto the I-90 on-ramp.

"The Devil I believe in. He's everywhere. Just go to a mall." Ran laughed.

"Why do you think the devil is a man?"

"Because men can't control their impulses."

With Ran rocking back and forth in the driver's seat, and Yuki feeding off his energy, they traded life stories.

Ran was from a wealthy white suburb near Wallingford in Connecticut.

"Would you believe that when I stepped off the train at West Glacier I was fat? I've probably lost thirty pounds."

Yuki told him details of her life, leaving out Minidoka and the rape, concentrating on Mel and Alice. She told him about the cancer, and that she was on her last trip. To visit 'someone in Idaho' is how she put it.

"It must be a special friend," said Ran, "to give them your last bit of time."

June 19

RAN DROVE HER, WITH some navigational difficulty, to her mother's grave. He'd waited politely in
the car while she walked the thirty feet or so to the flat
gravestone. Around the stone the grass was mowed
and vibrated with sun green. Small flags, flowers, and
gifts adorned neighboring graves. The sun was high,
the cemetery perched on a bluff overlooking Flathead
Lake. The Lake seemed to stretch forever into the
distance, a dance of gold and blue. Several power
boats cut the water, leaving white wakes on the
turquoise water.

Yuki stared down at the stone. The simple
inscription cut into white granite of the small haka
read Mizuki Kuneto 1911 – 1991 "Life is a Wonder."
It was something her mother would say all the time.
Her mother's friends often told Yuki that Mizuki had
lived long enough to possess wisdom. Even at the end,
when she was worn down by arthritis and cancer, she
would still beam her smile at people and say, "Life is
a wonder." Yuki had hoped she would be as life-
affirming and noble at the end of her own life. On the
other hand, she knew the complexities of her mother's
life, and knew her mother's optimism and "niceness"

was often her taught cultural politeness. Yuki accepted the fact she was different, more American, less polite. But also, perhaps, less self-assured and confident of her place in a larger structure.

For the second time today, Yuki found herself praying. This time she began talking to her mother as if she were there, telling her about the gulls sitting on the railing to her left, and the mountains and clouds mirrored in the lake; how brilliant green the grass was, and how that caused her heart to ache. And finally, how much Yuki missed her, and how much she would miss Alice. Bowing slightly, Yuki said "I hope I will see you soon." It felt like a true prayer.

She'd bought Ran lunch at a small downtown cafe in Polson, and watched him wolf mammoth quantities of pickles and French fries while downing two bowls of chili and a bacon blue-cheese burger. Yuki munched on lettuce. Somehow, in spite of the fact that Ran's mouth was overflowing with food, it also seemed capable of overflowing with endless, interloping narrative, focusing on life's mission and purpose, which apparently included a lot of fuel, when he could get it.

Ran pulled into a gas station immediately off the Orange Street exit in Missoula around 4:30 in the afternoon.

"You need gas," he said as he popped the cap and jumped out, sticking the nozzle into the tank hole, pushing the regular option. Yuki got out of the car.

"Well I guess this is it. You gave me a wonderful gift, Ran. Thank you."

She gave Ran a hug, which he returned, holding her so tightly she could barely breathe. Yuki began to struggle against his strength and bulk, panicked. But he didn't let go. "Relax, Yuki. Relax. Let it go. Let it all go. The fear, the cancer, everything."

Yuki fought a moment longer, then surrendered. She hung shivering, crying and shaking in this big kid's embrace. Only later did she remember the difficulty she'd had relaxing when Mel held her. She remembered being held down by the guards at Minidoka. It had been after that she'd torn away from her mother's hugs. She wouldn't surrender to anyone, be held tightly by anyone, not even her daughter, her husband. Ran had broken that resistance, operating on instinct and prayer.

After a minute or so, the sun hot on her shoulders, she said, "Now you can let go."

He did, and laughed. "It's hard, isn't it? Letting go. But we have to. We all have to."

He stood there in the full-blooming day with an off-kilter grin and a slight wave, his mammoth pack towering over his shoulders. And Yuki felt the stab of loneliness as he walked off. His friends lived only a few blocks away, he told her, and he wanted to walk.

Yuki paid for the gas and returned to her car. Then she followed the directions the clerk had given her to a nearby motel.

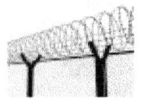

Yesterday had exhausted Yuki. She lay in bed after waking the next morning and stared at light leaking under the curtain. She had no will to move. Her clothes stuck to her from when she'd curled in the bed late the previous afternoon. She hadn't taken any pills in over twenty-four hours. Her body was frayed with pain, her muscles burning. Her stomach housed a fire that flared at will. The serpent grinned at her. He knew he had her.

After what seemed like hours, she finally rolled over and neatly vomited bile into a trash can, wiping her mouth with the sheet as she tried to sit up. The pain in her gut did its best to push her back. It took a few turns, but she succeeded, then swung her legs over the side of the bed. They felt rubbery and floppy as she tried to walk. It took holding onto the bed, then a few yards of tottering over carpet with her arms waving for balance, but she finally made it over to a window. She pulled up the curtain and pushed the window open, cracking her reflection in half.

A glass of water later she watched steaming water pour from a stainless-steel faucet into a pink bathtub. It was the first time she'd used a bar to lower herself into the water, but every day seemed to hand her another first. As she eased into the water, Yuki forced herself to confront the scarred terrain of her stomach and lower abdomen — a web of leering rubbery welts that represented her last violation. Her breasts, tiny as they were, sagged, and pulled at the loose skin of her chest. She hadn't weighed herself in over a month and was scared to. Her legs, her pride really, along with her strong, open face, were always muscular. Now they were sticks with sagging gray flesh clinging dearly to them. "This is no time for self-pity," she said out loud, throwing the bar of soap at the wall. And she forced a laugh.

The bath rejuvenated her somewhat, and

afterwards Yuki sat on the bed to towel herself off. Over the past few months, pain was a filial companion, seldom far from her side. Medication kept it a blurry buzz, but without her meds it flared, bright and hot. She put her hand to her stomach. She knew from this point on she would use her pain to focus her, to wake her, to keep her alive.

Outside the window cottonwood leaves flickered with sun then shade. Yuki watched an oriole alight, then disappear into its nest, a woven sac hanging just outside the window. She hobbled over but couldn't see the opening. She knew from the insect in the bird's beak that young life huddled inside. Her longing to be near Alice hit her hard, as it had several times already. Despite Alice's begging, Yuki had left her phone behind. The phone, and the connections it offered, were part of what Yuki needed to shed as she moved into her final stage. Yuki hadn't left Alice in good graces. Alice was upset with her foolishness, and had practically cursed her. But there were things Alice did not yet understand. And Yuki needed to face this alone.

She dug some crackers out of a shopping bag and chewed, tasting salt and nothing else as she turned on the TV, bouncing through channels for a few minutes, then snapped it off. There was more bad news outside this room than inside it, but that didn't make her feel any better. She finished another cracker, brushed her hands together, then fished the card out of her purse.

Kathy Riordan, the woman professor she'd met in Hawaii.

Yuki had felt a deep connection as they talked on the breakfast terrace of the Queen Kapiolani Hotel.

She picked up the phone but couldn't get a dial tone. No matter, she'd call her from the lobby.

Oddly, she felt hungrier after the crackers. Downstairs there was a pancake house that spanned a creek, and Yuki settled herself into a booth next to the window. She watched the water boil turbulent underneath her. Light stunned and fractured as it broke over the rocks and flushed to foam. Its blind obedience to gravity and the laws of physics amazed her, and she thought if only I could lose myself like that, if only I were blind to myself the way water is. A robin flew across the stream and landed in an alder, cocked its head and stared straight at her. She remembered the pine marten she'd seen yesterday, the way it looked at her, as if inviting her into its world.

Yuki ordered tea, toast, and a wedge of cantaloupe. The waitress brought it with a smile, but Yuki could see curiosity in her eyes. Bald Japanese women on their last legs were less common in Montana than Seattle, not that they were common there either. But she smiled back, and the waitress looked relieved and asked if there was anything else? She remembered how her mother defined a smile as "Giving light," and she shook her head.

The melon was the first food she'd really tasted in months and it nearly exploded in her mouth. It made her gasp, and the waitress, a college student Yuki assumed, turned and asked her again if there was anything else she needed.

"This melon is so good!"

"We just got the shipment in. It's from Mexico." The waitress looked pleased, and said, "I'm glad you're enjoying it."

What a simple gift, Yuki thought. How I would have taken all this for granted not so long ago.

Yuki finished her breakfast, charging it to her room. In the lobby she told the desk clerk her phone was broken. The young woman said she'd already reported it, and Yuki could use the one behind the desk.

Yuki dialed the number on Kathy's card. The phone rang several times then a woman answered.

"Kathy Riordan." Her voice brought back the sunny, breezy terrace of the restaurant in Honolulu.

"Hi. My name is Yuki. I met you in Hawaii at breakfast at my hotel. The Queen Kapiolani? You were at a conference, and I mentioned I might be traveling this way. You gave me your card."

The woman laughed. "I do remember! What a surprise! Where are you?"

"I'm in town. At the Creekside Motor Inn. I'm passing through on my way to Idaho and I thought, well, I wanted to see you."

"Great, that would be great! I'm in my office and I've got students here, but later would be fine."

"Should I come by your office?"

"How about dinner? You could come over to my house. Do you have a car?"

"Yes. But I can't eat much. Between the cancer and the chemo my stomach and intestines have been slaughtered."

Yuki heard concern deepen Kathy's voice. "I'll make something mild. Trout and rice. My students are always giving me trout."

"That actually sounds good. Fish is one food that usually stays down."

"I'll keep it mild. Butter on the side. Here's the address. 313 Beckwith. It's just west of the University. Where are you staying again?"

"The Creekside Motor Inn."

"Okay, that's easy." Kathy gave Yuki instructions from her hotel. "How about six o'clock?"

"Great. I'll be there. Should I bring anything?"

"No, no, just bring yourself." She paused and said, "It will be good to see you."

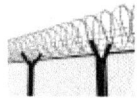

With her cane, which Yuki was becoming more and more dependent on, she walked slower, and noticed that people moved aside for her. I could move here and become a strange character in a novel, she thought. Nobody would know me. I could be somebody who suddenly appears, then disappears when the page is turned.

Yuki found a wonderful little coffee shop that felt like stepping back into the sixties. Several students walked by her smelling of patchouli. Maybe hippies were coming back. Or maybe they'd never left Missoula. The tea, a local blend, tasted wonderful, and she indulged herself with a refill.

After walking through downtown, Yuki found a trail along the Clark's Fork River, which meandered through town, corralled by rocky, cottonwood lined shores. Two young men were fly-fishing off a cobble bar, their peach line arcing across the current and drifting down. They retrieved the flies with short jerks and casted again. Yuki sat and watched them, their graceful movements, their repetition. They seemed satisfied not catching a fish, simply existing on the river, casting. The sun felt delicious, and Yuki watched the river flow past, and deep serenity entered her.

She woke with a start, not knowing exactly how much time had passed, but noting the shadows slanted further to the east. The fishermen were gone, replaced by a great blue heron, and the river still flowed west toward Seattle and home. Home – such a strange word. Yuki knew she'd never see her condo in Queen Anne again. She felt her life draining from her, sometimes quickly, sometimes more slowly. She was a vessel whose water or wine was being poured out into the soil. She would lose herself soon. Ran's words echoed in her ears. "We all have to let go." There was no arguing with it. And then she smiled, and thought of her mother. "Giving light."

Sitting, staring at the river, she tried to tap her anger toward Devin Richter. It was the origin and purpose of this trip, but here she felt like the wind, the water, and the chiaroscuro of the cottonwood shadows and sun had blurred or hidden it. The fact she could even be here, could witness this beauty, all conspired against her wishes. The memory of the girl being pushed to the floor in the warehouse seemed like a faded photograph of someone she'd known long ago but hadn't seen in years. She got up and slowly walked back to her motel.

Showers felt so good these days. She felt lighter after each one, as if she dispelled flesh along with dirt and sweat. She was becoming pure air, pure light. She dressed in a faded blue cotton sundress. She'd brought only a few clothes with her, and they were all worn-out old favorites.

A breeze had leapt up, and Yuki had goose-bumps before she reached the car.

Sitting behind the wheel she stared at her stick-like arms, the tiny bumps rippling them. 'Who is this frail thing?' she wondered. Her body no longer belonged to her. The auto suddenly felt too large for her, like a spaceship with a dashboard of unfamiliar command buttons. Yuki got out of the car, walked back into motel lobby, took a peppermint out of the crystal bowl on the desk and placed it on her tongue. She asked the polite, copper-wire haired boy behind the desk to call her a cab.

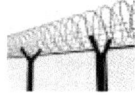

The cabbie helped her out of the cab, and Yuki set off down the sidewalk with her cane. Kathy's house was a small bungalow with a large screened-in front porch. Lilacs were still blooming in the late spring, hanging like heavy pomes of fruit. Yuki cupped one of them and inhaled. It made her delirious.

The front door was open and Yuki heard music that reminded her of life before the camps — ceremonies replete with diverse food, parents dancing, and the secret life of children under tables and through legs. The jazz of big bands that she and Mel had fallen in love with again while taking ballroom dance classes. Paul Whiteman, Glenn Miller, Benny Goodman, Tommy Dorsey.

She rang the bell several times before deciding that Kathy, who she saw in the kitchen, couldn't hear it above the music. Shuffling into the living room, Yuki watched Kathy slicing vegetables while she swayed to the happy rhythms. Yuki set the sake she'd brought down on the counter and smiled as Kathy turned to her.

Kathy's face registered surprise, then light.

"I didn't hear you." She opened her arms wide for a hug.

She embraced Yuki and Yuki could smell lilacs on her.

"God you're a wisp of a thing. Are you sure this is alright?"

"This is the best thing I can imagine," Yuki replied. She waved the cane in the air. "Check out my new leg."

"A nice one, I'd say. Sturdy. You didn't have that in Hawaii, did you?"

"No." Then after a hesitation, "I brought it from home.

Kathy stood back and gave Yuki an appraising look. "What do you have?"

"Cancer. Pancreatic cancer."

"You poor dear. Have a seat."

Kathy pulled a wooden chair out from the table and Yuki sat down.

"I wondered, when we met in Hawaii. Your hair." Kathy ran her hand over her own hair. "You asked me something about death, if I recall. Are you very sick?"

"Overall, yes. Some days are better than others. This is a good one. I've started getting my taste back, and whatever I eat tastes wonderful. I want to eat and eat and eat but I can't because my stomach is all screwed up."

"Well, I hope you like what I'm cooking. It's a rainbow trout, given to me by one of my students. He caught it right outside town. My students like to take care of me. I must project helplessness." She laughed.

"It is such a beautiful day." Kathy gestured toward the living room where a couple of loveseats intersected. "Let's sit in there for a while, let the vegetables take care of themselves." She picked up the saki. "Should I?"

"Sure," Yuki said. "I'd love some." Looking around, "You have a lovely home. It's so simple, yet intimate. I was a realtor in my former life, and the easiest places to sell were houses that reflected an owner's love of them."

"Thank you. It's small, comfortable and cute. And I've lived here far too long to give it up." She had an easy laugh. "So, you were a realtor? You did well for yourself?"

"I did. I had a wonderful life in retrospect, though very different from the movie."

"Oh yes, Jimmy Stewart. It used to be required Christmas viewing."

Kathy handed Yuki a small glass and settled herself into one of the loveseats and patted the cushion next to her. Yuki sat down.

"You live alone?"

"I have for years. Oh, I take in the occasional homeless college student, but for the most part it's just me. Oh, and Kitty, who you might see later."

"I have a cat in Seattle. Her name is Kitso." She took a sip of saki and it warmed her as it went down.

She shivered involuntarily.

"Are you okay?"

"Yes. It's good isn't it?"

"Yes. I rarely drink sake. There's not much Asian culture here."

"I like the town, though. And the weather." Yuki laughed. "You've probably heard all the stories of our gray and rain. Well they're all true."

"Summer in Montana and a lovely dinner guest. Life is good indeed." Kathy laughed, and they sat as her laugh faded and the music again asserted itself.

"Were you ever married?" Yuki glanced at a wall of photographs and postcards.

"I was, but he left me years ago. He still lives in town. Remarried. I never did. We're friends."

"My husband died several years ago. It was a dark time for me."

"I can imagine. So, are you just traveling through?"

"In a manner of speaking, yes. Traveling through my life." Yuki thought of Ran and smiled. "I'm going to Idaho to see someone."

"Oh, how nice. A friend? Family?"

"Nothing so pleasant, I'm afraid. I'm going to talk to a man who raped me when I was a child. I was in an internment camp in Idaho. Minidoka Camp. He was a guard. There were two of them, but the older man died. Devin," she coughed demurely, "that's his name, is living in a nursing home. He's in bad shape."

Kathy stared at Yuki, her green eyes catching the evening slant of sun. "What an extraordinary journey. It sounds difficult. Mythic." Her voice choked with emotion. "And you're dying, aren't you? You won't come back from this." It wasn't a question. "This is truly your last journey."

Yuki poured another glass of sake. "You'll have to pardon me. I get sick sometimes. It happens quickly."

"Let me get a wastebasket."

Yuki watched Kathy carry a basket over, looking up at her like a small child.

"So, you don't think I'm crazy?"

"No way. I think you're heroic. You're going to battle your demon. I couldn't do what you're doing."

"My daughter thinks I'm crazy. She thinks I should go into a home and let some hospice nurse pump me full of morphine while I watch old movies." Yuki laughed. "I feel so good sometimes. I mean I'm in constant pain, often brutal pain, but I feel almost ecstatic."

"You are free, Yuki. You're living. It's crazy that you, or anyone, has to get next to death to live, but it's so often true. Many religions teach this. Death is revered and made deliberately conscious in many religions. Catholicism with their ever-present crucifixes, Buddhism with ego death, letting go of the self, Kali in Hinduism. The list goes on. Our culture, however, spiritually bereft as it is, is death denying. And ironically, life-denying as well." She laughed. "I'm sorry, I'm sounding like a professor, aren't I? It's habitual."

"It's fine. It's why I came. I felt you could teach me."

"Au contraire dear, you can teach me. Should we tackle the trout, pardon the pun? Another fault of mine."

Yuki nibbled at her trout and vegetables and the tastes were profound. She wanted to stuff her mouth, but she could already feel her stomach contracting. They finished the bottle of sake and Kathy opened some delicious chardonnay, which they began drinking too liberally.

"Why did you decide to teach religion?" Yuki asked at one point.

"I became fascinated by the fact that almost, if not all cultures had some form of worship. Which meant they believed there existed something greater than themselves. What that was, and how it manifested, varied of course, but that's a pretty remarkable human trait. The desire to fear, or praise, something larger. I read a lot when I was young, and I found that more and more of what I was reading had to do with religion in that sense. Praising something larger and greater than oneself. Believe it or not, I was originally going to be a high school math teacher. I still love mathematics."

"So, are you religious? Or is your involvement solely academic?" Yuki pushed some zucchini around with her fork.

"I was born Catholic, and after a long traipse down a path that could generously be called Buddhist, I've returned."

"Why?"

Kathy laughed. "Good question. But basically, I became more tolerant and less judgmental of it. Any religion is easy to critique, but that's its human nature. Religions are paths toward something. They are processes that one voluntarily joins. And that's where faith comes in. Believing enough to join in."

"We met because of faith, you remember, don't you? Your conference was about faith."

"That's right." Kathy laughed. "Faith does great things doesn't it? It brought us together."

Yuki was silent for too long, staring at her wine glass. "I wish I had faith in something."

"What do you want to have faith in?" Kathy asked. Her smile had disappeared.

'Oh, you know, life after death. God. Love. I think my rape as a child brought a darkness into my life that I couldn't shake, but never really examined. I remember deciding, because my parents were very religious, very Protestant, I remember deciding there could not be a God, at least not a loving one, because no God could ever allow that to happen to a little girl."

"That's one of the hardest doubts. Some Christians would argue that the men who raped you will suffer an eternal hell. Others…"

Yuki interrupted. "Unless they asked forgiveness, right? Isn't that the trump card in all religions? If they are repentant before they die, they are saved and go to any number of cool eternal pastures. Because that's what a Christian God does. But what about the victim? Can I ask forgiveness for her too?" Yuki began to cry.

"Honey, come here." Kathy got up and bent over Yuki, hugging her.

Yuki wasn't sure how it happened, but Kathy lifted her from the chair, still crying, and guided her into a small peach-colored bedroom. She laid Yuki on the bed, lay her down, and lay down next to her, stroking her hair, and then holding her. Yuki's body shook with grief, an overarching grief she had never allowed herself to know: the grief of being raped, of her husband Mel's death, her mother's death, of the young boy in Honolulu, of herself dying, giving up her body, emptying herself into vast space. And then it was more than grief, it was joy as well. The joy of her marriage day, of giving birth to Alice, of the beautiful sunsets that had drawn tears to her eyes, the wounded thrush she had held in her hands, its eye's precious stone cutting into her. And her cat Kitso, her softest purr while she kneaded Yuki's stomach, such joy. And such loss. And un-nameables, as infinite as stars.

"Life is so transient," she said to Kathy through her tears, "so beautiful."

She fell asleep in Kathy's arms. She dreamt she was walking down a narrow gravel road through a forest of tall fir. It was daylight, but sun didn't strike the road. She could hear her footsteps crunch the gravel, and the fading light spawned a breeze and chilled her. Walking, she heard the whisper of feathers, all those words we never quite hear. And then she walked with a man and woman next to her, each taking her hand in theirs. Their wings white as virgin snow. They said nothing. They simply walked, holding Yuki's hands. And Yuki felt she was ascending, that pressure was building, tightening its hands around her skull, her chest, her abdomen, pressing, pressing. Then everything erupted, she was blown apart, pain dissipating into vast space, infinite particles in infinite winds, and then an enormous sense of peace....

She woke to Kathy, fully dressed and coated, ready to leave apparently, kissing her softly on the lips.

"Do you believe in angels?" Yuki asked her.

Kathy looked at her strangely, then smiled. "Yes, of course I do. You are an angel." She put her hand on Yuki's forehead. "I have to go. I really enjoyed our time together. Help yourself to breakfast, anything. The door locks when you close it. I wish you the best in your journey."

June 21

YUKI DROVE SOUTH INTO the Bitterroot Valley, leaving Missoula and its sprawl behind by mid-morning. By the time she hit Stevensville the air was choked with rusty smoke smeared by faint sun. Even with the windows up Yuki felt she was choking. Her wipers clawed at a faint residue of ash. Forest fires above the valley. She was choking and her anger once again swarmed.

She had lunch in a small café in Victor and listened to a table of ranchers criticize everything from the government to the snowpack. She ordered a chocolate malt and made it a quarter-way through before she felt it coming back up. She stared at herself in the bathroom mirror and forced herself to smile. She was valiant but she knew she was losing.

Yuki pulled into the gravel lot of a small green rectangular building that advertised GUNS on the white warped plastic marquee. The anger had cooled to pain, a steady vein that fed her.

She told the man behind the gun counter that she was traveling across the country, and while napping at a rest area a man had tried to get in the car. She was remembering the state trooper in Idaho. Her fear waking up with him looming outside, rapping on her window.

The man behind the counter had a round reddened face and a white mustache. His sizable belly made it difficult for him to get too close to the counter. His blue eyes twinkled.

"That must have been terrifying." He looked her up and down. "You're just a little thing, aren't you ma'am." It wasn't a question but a statement of the obvious. "You need something small. A little .38 like this one." The man reached into the case and pulled out a pistol. It was chrome with a black plastic handle. She took it from his hand. It was heavier than she expected.

"This here is a Smith and Wesson snub-nosed thirty-eight. It would be perfect for someone your size."

She turned her hands and held it sideways, then even, straight ahead.

"You ever shot a handgun before?"

"My husband took me shooting a couple of times. I didn't like it."

"Too noisy, huh? Well this little baby will pack a wallop. But mostly, all's ya gotta do is flash it at someone and they'll head the other direction. No man in his right mind wants to mess with someone who's armed."

Yuki was quiet.

"Can I see a photo ID? Driver's License, somethin like that?"

Yuki fished in her purse and handed the man her license. His hand practically engulfed her hand and the license. He had enormous hands. His mustache was startlingly white.

"My name's Marvin, by the way. I own this shop." He was squinting at the license. "You ain't from here are you? This says Washington State."

"That's right. I'm from Seattle. I'm driving down to visit someone in Idaho."

"We got a problem then, lady. I can't sell handguns to anyone who lives out of state. You have to be a Montana resident to buy a handgun legally in Montana."

"I'm not a criminal. I haven't ever committed a crime."

"And I'm sure you don't intend to. No ma'am, this is a predicament. I could sell you one of these pellet guns." He waved at a display of pistols to his left. "They look real enough. Might scare a man off if he don't know nothing about guns." He handed her back the license.

Yuki shook her head, then she shivered violently.

"This fellow shook you up pretty good, didn't he?"

She nodded.

"You call the police?"

She looked at him blankly.

"When the guy tried to get into your car. You call the police after?"

"No. Someone pulled into the rest area and scared him off."

"This happen in Montana?"

"No. Over in Idaho. In a rest area by Coeur d'Alene."

"You should never never ever sleep in no rest area, ma'am. Even I wouldn't do that. It's just askin for trouble."

"I was tired. It was night. I was just going to take a nap."

The man grunted and put his large hand over his white mustache and kept it there.

"Look, I've been thinking about this. I can't sell you none of this here inventory legally, cause I gotta keep records of everything. The feds be on my butt if I don't have proper records. But I could sell you a private gun, me to you, see? There wouldn't be no paperwork."

He picked up the .38 and cradled it in his palm. "This here's like the gun my wife owned before she died. It's the same gun as this one here, cept older. But it works great. There's no problem with it. I'll even let you shoot it. We'd have to drive back to my house though. I'd sell you that gun for two hundred dollars. That's a hell of a savings to you, as this one here is around eight hundred."

"You would do that?"

"Sure. I got no use for the damned gun. It's a lady's gun. It's just stuck in a drawer with a bunch of my wife's stuff I ain't sorted out yet." The man reached under the counter. "Here, let me hang this sign on the door and we'll be on our way." The sign read GONE FISHING. "I'm just a few minutes out of town." He opened the door for Yuki and let her out.

"I'll make a U-turn here, then you just follow me. Be there before you know it."

Yuki followed the truck down the highway until Marvin turned hard right, skidding his F-350 on gravel up a sharp hill, and she followed. He waited for her on the plateau, and Yuki saw the fields, dotted with cattle and hay, roll west to the snow-covered mountains. She followed him another two miles to a squat farm house surrounded by cottonwoods.

She waited on the porch even though he invited her in. She held onto the railing, staring across a field of alfalfa, incredibly green. She wanted to surrender herself to that green and never return.

The screen door slammed, and the man walked toward her with the pistol. He held it out to her. Leaning against the railing for balance, she took the gun from him.

"It's loaded and ready to go. I've got some targets. I'll put one on a hay bale back here, and you can get the feel of it." He walked around the house on a driveway and Yuki followed, holding the gun in one hand, jamming her cane into the hard earth with the other. A shed and a half-painted barn stood to the left. Marvin headed over there. Despite the heat of a summer day her hand that held the gun felt very cold. She let out a long breath and tried to raise it, but the gun's weight was enormous.

Marvin walked to the end of the barn and disappeared, returning a moment later with a bale of golden hay. He stacked four of these, lengthwise, then went into the shed, returning, carrying a life-size black and white silhouette which he attached to the bales.

"Okay, now wait until I'm back here, and we'll put this bad guy down."

She used the cane on her right hip, leaning into it, stabilizing, the gun at her side, pain coming blind. She grimaced. If Marvin noticed he didn't say anything.

"Okay. This is a good distance, about twenty feet. You don't want to be shooting at anything farther away than this. Let him have it."

Yuki again tried to raise the gun, but again its weight was too much. Then anger seized her, white hot anger, and she saw Devin, his head as it had been that night, above her, and without thinking she had the gun up and fired five times in quick succession, the report smacking her ears, then fading as she lowered the gun. Her arm was shaking and she dropped the gun to the ground.

"Looks like you did some damage, little lady. Let's go see."

The target was intact with the exception of the silhouette's forehead, which was erased, amber hay erupting from the holes like stiff wild hair.

The man raised his hand toward the woman, as if blessing her, but said nothing.

Then he spoke, sputtering a bit.

"Lady…lady! Jesus, I hope I can trust you lady. You ain't some Asian mafia gal, are you?"

Yuki stared at the ground.

"Husband used to take you out huh?"

Yuki couldn't speak.

Marvin palmed his chin, then said "Take the gun, lady. There's no charge. I don't know what you plan to do with it, but you have my blessing."

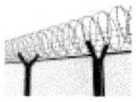

Yuki pulled onto a gravel shoulder at the top of Lost Trail Pass. The air was clear and clean and her anger had calmed. Her moods were so labile lately, she was blown through by wind, burned by fire, erased by clouds.

With the window open, and jays squawking, she leaned the seat back and closed her eyes. It was warm and flies buzzed in and out, the wind flickered through the Lodgepole Pine. She started drifting off, then snapped awake. She thought someone had called her. Two jays were bickering outside. She drifted off again.

Yuki dreamed herself walking by a river, its slate-green water covered with fluorescent green and orange pill bottles. She began running through the shallow water, trying to scoop them and throw them onto the shore. When she had a pile of them, she noticed they were all empty. She walked on. As she came around the river's bend, a gathering of crows on the cobble spooked, and spooked her, and she tripped. She remembered going down, a sharp pain in her knee as it hit the rocks, then she was out.

Yuki awakened in a room at the Minidoka Camp. The room was barren, the plywood walls scraped raw, the plank floor rough. Cold wind stormed the cracks and Yuki realized she was naked. Suddenly the door opened and Devin Richter entered. He stood over her, his eyes vacant, and began unbuttoning his pants. Yuki couldn't move. He roughly pulled her legs apart and pushed himself into her. Yuki felt like she was being ripped in two, and Devin's face came closer, his eyes bloodshot, the edges of his mouth curled away from his teeth. Yuki was collapsing into herself, imploding, becoming dark, darker, losing consciousness. And then from some miraculous fount of strength she fought back, attempting to roll to the side, then reaching up with her hand to grab Devin's hair, then the skin of his face, his cheek. And in that moment his face came off in her hand, and behind it was only sky devoid of clouds. And she found herself a little girl, aged four or five, lying on a grassy patch in a park near their Seattle home staring up at the sky. And she heard her mother's voice calling her name, "Yuki, Yuki," calling her home.

When Yuki woke it was to a body that was no longer hers, although it burned with pain. She was steeped in sweat and had wet herself. She began crying, but softly steeled herself. Retrieving them from the car, she awkwardly changed her pants and underpants while a pine squirrel chattered at her angrily. When she again settled into the driver's seat a sense of calm had engulfed her. She started the car and drove into Idaho, following the serpentine highway down the valley to the Salmon River.

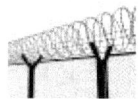

She stayed that night at a wooden lodge near Salmon that had an indoor hot springs pool. The lodge, a spacious wooden structure built in the early 1900s, was relatively deserted. A small group of construction workers sat at the bar, their laughter exploding into the cavernous lobby. She checked in, and was handed a metal key to a first-floor room as she'd requested. Once in the room she immersed the soiled pants and underpants in the bathtub and scrubbed them with soap, hanging them on the shower curtain.

After a small salad and a lamb chop, which she

smeared with mint jelly, then couldn't eat, Yuki walked back through the lobby. The construction workers had gone elsewhere, and it was quiet. She opened the door that led to the pool.

Mel would have called it funky, and that would have added to its charm for him. The pool's age was apparent from the peeling paint, the algae, and the worn wooden deck. But steam rose languorously from the limpid water. The damp wooden walls gave off the smell of an old cedar sauna. Several naked bulbs overhead, their yellow auras adding to the silence, cast the only light.

Yuki walked halfway down the far side equidistant between two lights and stripped to her bra and panties, easing herself into the water. It nearly took her breath away. She felt a delirious, almost sexual warmth enter her. She couldn't touch bottom, and held onto the side closing her eyes. She had no idea how much time had passed when she heard a wooden door bang, and voices entered the room, a boy and girl goofing and pushing each other. They didn't notice her as she worked her way over to a ladder and climbed out. There was a sudden shriek as the girl hit the water, followed by laughter that bounced between the tepid damp walls. It was still there as Yuki left the room.

June 22

YUKI SLEPT IN, DRIFTING in and out of dream. Last night she had woken to coyotes yipping and howling. They sounded so close that she'd looked out the window, but saw only highway lit by mercury vapor lights from the general store. The sky was enormous and blown apart with stars. She was awake for a long time, twisting, trying to escape a pain that would not be shaken off.

There were only three other groups in the café as she devoured a bowl of oatmeal covered with strawberries. She knew she would throw it up but she didn't care. This must be what bulimics went through. Eating and vomiting it up. She supposed the body could get used to almost anything.

She was lucky, the waitress said. They'd just gotten fresh strawberries from Washington. Yuki thought this might be the last time she ever ate strawberries, and the thought pushed tears to her eyes. They had no tea, so she had a cup of coffee. It was hot and felt good on her throat. Yesterday's smoky air had parched it.

The day was brilliant. She drove through mountains, the Sawtooths, as she found out, stopping in Stanley for lunch, and thought it one of the most beautiful places on earth. Everything was rarified in the high-altitude light. Mountains capped with snow gleaming in the sun, and the river behind the restaurant dancing. The whole place left her aching for more.

The winding road climbed and climbed and the curves nauseated her, and she had to pull over several times. Gum helped, and she thought back on the strip of gum, Juicyfruit, Alice had handed her after picking her up after her last round of chemo. "Your favorite," she'd said. It seemed so long ago.

The road finally descended, broke out of the mountains onto high plains and straightened. She had the instructions her daughter had printed for her on the passenger's seat. Alice's printing hadn't changed since second or third grade, and Yuki felt time, like wind, blowing through her.

The landscape changed to fields of alfalfa, giant sprinklers on wheels, irrigation canals, and on undeveloped plots, dried grass and sagebrush. And then the sign for Jerome, and memories stirred within her. Yuki found it ironic that the turnoff from Highway 93 was called Eden. The Garden of Eden, home to her original sin.

There were no signs, but her daughter's directions were exact. Turning here, then on Hunt Road, she soon crossed the ditch, and there was some familiarity even though the nearly 600 buildings had been erased. It was a deliberate erasure, a country hiding its sins. Even the tall watchtowers were gone.

She pulled into a small parking lot surrounded by Russian olives and cottonwoods. A row of Lombardy poplar to her left, and willow by the great ditch. A few people had tried to swim in the ditch and some had drowned, so they dug a safe, benign swimming hole on the west side of the camp. All around her dry grass and sage stretched to the sky, and dark mountains smudged the distance. The area was vast and desolate, but all at once she heard a cacophony of voices, all speaking Japanese, and the wind kicked up the dust of ghosts. She closed her eyes and saw many faces, and arms reaching out for her. Then as suddenly as it came, it was gone.

Yuki got out of the car and confronted the crumbling, hulking stone fireplace of the entry building. Constructed of black lava rock, Yuki remembered giant logs sparking and giving off waves of heat in the frigid winters. Now there was only stillness. It seemed a place far from humanity. Birds were calling, and the mountains to the north and southeast were mute.

She wandered the several paths that curled from the entryway, swatting at swarms of flies that descended on her. She hadn't remembered the flies. Had they even been there then? Numerous swallows wove the air over the big ditch, and she recognized some of the birdcalls – red-winged blackbirds, meadowlarks.

Upwards of 13,000 people had lived here, in this harsh place of no remorse. They had dug ditches, irrigated the rich volcanic loam, planted seeds, nursed plants into the months of blazing sun, and harvested the crops. Seeds enough for next year. For nearly three years the camp had carried nearly the entire agricultural output of the area. Where had the profit gone, Yuki wondered? Who had gotten rich off their backs?

Yuki remembered her father talking with them after dinner. He'd light a pipe, and as an unwritten rule, no one was allowed to leave until he finished his talk and his pipe. Her brother called them sermons. And they were full of warnings, and as he spoke, in short staccato bursts, he would point the stem of his pipe at them one by one. But Yuki defended him. She thought him wise. She still did.

One evening he said, "You know we would do the same thing to the Americans."

No one challenged him, and it added to our resignation.

But there were those who didn't accept their fate, those who fought back. People were removed and never heard from again. Petitions circulated. Men whispered in the lanes outside the auras of light. In 1944, male prisoners were given the chance to join the American army. Those that didn't, faced potential punishment, though of what nature was vague. Her father had refused, and after several worrisome weeks, was given a deferment because of his age and family.

As she walked, the camp rose from dust. She saw the barracks, the groups of kids playing with balls and sticks. In the monotony of those camp days, the memory of her rape gradually slipped below the surface. But when she saw Devin walk by one evening and smile at her, she knew she would never forget. That the memory, in decomposing, had entered her soil, her structure, and everything that grew out of her would be tainted. Her escape was to work without stopping, to drown her memory in activity. The hardest had been the baseball games. She had to continually fabricate excuses to miss Bobby's games. It seemed a small thing, but in the architecture of the camp, it drove a wedge between them, and in time he stopped asking. After the camp, they were never again close. And she never told him why.

Yuki felt silence pound in her ears and sweat soaked her. Dizzy, she sat on a log that bordered the trail. Swallows wheeled above her in abstract mathematics she could appreciate without understanding. 'I won't live much longer," she said out loud, "I have to settle this."

The quick buzz startled her as she walked back to her car, and looking down she saw the snake, its girth coiled under itself, head balanced, tongue tasting the air. Yuki hopped backwards, her cane skittering towards the snake which struck at it, then fled. Yuki landed heavily, cutting her left calf on the igneous rock. Petrified, she stared at the crack the snake had disappeared into, finally getting the nerve to retrieve her cane and push herself up. Her heart pounded as if to finally escape its fragile cage.

It took Yuki forty minutes to get into Twin Falls. She pulled into a Quality Inn motel on the right after she crossed the bridge over a canyon with the Snake River slithering far below. She checked in and fell onto the bed, waking nine hours later. She refused to get up, winding through dreams and voices calling out to her. She heard her mother again calling her home. She was in a frigid sweat, the air conditioner blasting her. Finally, she dragged herself up.

She gripped the bar tightly in the shower, letting hot water soak into her ravaged body. She could see death. It was a happy mask of gossamer that hung in front of whatever she glanced at. Not dark exactly. More like the shadow of a shadow. She tried to catch it, but death was slippery. It would not yet commit.

She asked the young woman at the desk how to get to the Cottonwood Nursing Home. It turned out to be only eight blocks. Four blocks on Blue Lake, then a left on Ninth. She walked cautiously back to her room and phoned an order for room service, but fell asleep before it came and didn't hear the bouts of knocking.

June 23

RAIN POUNDED THE ASPHALT of the parking lot. Yuki let the curtain fall back in place and phoned for two eggs, melon, and tea. Then she stood under the shower and felt the rain. This was the day.

Yuki was sitting on the bed watching a morning news show when her breakfast arrived. She ate hurriedly, the heavily salted soft-boiled eggs dissolving in her mouth while the melon exploded, musky and sweet. Scraping her plate, she was suddenly queasy, and made it to the toilet just in time. Her sickness would only allow her tea today. She glanced in the mirror then stared in horror at what stared back. The serpent was in her, grinning. She let out a short scream, and then it was only her alone with the wreck of her body. The snake had retreated again. And then as she stared, she began to fill with light. She became beautiful to herself.

"I love you, Yuki," she said to herself in the mirror, and she saw her mirror image say it back.

She took her time with her modest make-up, giving her face color, her cheeks a pale flush, her lips a blush. She positioned the wig for the first time in over a month. She placed the gun into her purse and covered it with a small scarf. She reviewed the directions the desk clerk had jotted down.

The rain had eased, but the desk girl asked if she had an umbrella, then lent her one. At 10:40 the morning traffic was light.

The Cottonwood Nursing Home was an older brick one-story building surrounded by arbor vitae, mugo pine and pyracantha. The front double doors were heavy, and after struggling for a moment Yuki pushed the blue automatic door button, listening to the door grind and stutter open. The lobby was hexagonal with hallways spoking off it. The sand-colored linoleum was worn and stained, the beige walls depressing and gouged. Several patients were in wheelchairs, and staff in scrubs moved about. A woman stood watering one of several sorry-looking potted plants.

"She's been trying to kill that plant for months and I think she's finally succeeding," said the smiling young woman at the reception desk. "Agnes, leave that plant alone."

Yuki asked if Devin Richter was in.

"Devin Richter," the woman repeated, flipping pages in a spiral-bound book.

"He's being washed, but you can see him in fifteen to twenty minutes."

"That would be fine."

"Can I tell him who wants to see him?"

"My name is Yuki."

"Last name?"

"Waldren."

The woman wrote it carefully into a notebook. "You can have a seat over in the waiting area. I'll call you when he's ready."

The waiting area was filled with chrome and polyester furniture, and small wooden tables overflowing with magazines, very few of them recent. Yuki sat down heavily, feeling the weight of her pain, of the gun in her purse. Her heart was beating too fast again, and for a moment she felt herself slipping away, but the sound of voices shouting from a bulky Magnavox TV brought her back. The people on the screen were distorted and the entire picture was covered with a pink glow. Yuki got up and fiddled with the knobs until people opened their mouths and nothing came out. Sitting again, she opened a ruffled People magazine. Muted sounds came to her sporadically but it was largely quiet. An older lady clomped her walker into the room at one point and looked around, saying, "I thought they said..." her voice trailing off, then she turned and clacked her walker out. Yuki could see through the windows across the lobby that the rain had stopped, and it was getting lighter. She suddenly felt very tired and lay back against the couch.

"Mrs. Waldron." Yuki woke with a start. She didn't know where she was, then saw the receptionist, several feet away, and heard her name. Yuki tried to rise, and the receptionist moved to help her up.

"You can see Mr. Richter now. I've let him know you're here."

"What did he say?"

The nurse whose name tag read Rose, shook her head and smiled. "He doesn't understand much. You'll see." Then she told Yuki to follow her.

They walked down the far hallway to the left of the lobby, then took a right fork. The open doors offered Yuki glimpses of hospital beds, televisions, small tables, and people waiting to die.

Devin Richter sat in a wheelchair dressed in a red flannel bathrobe full of tiny dragons, open, exposing the top of his chest. A wooden crucifix on a gold chain perched on silver curls of chest hair. His head was tipped to the side as if carried adrift by its weight, and a thread of saliva stretched from his mouth to his shoulder, where it formed a large damp spot.

"He had a stroke several months ago and sometimes he can't talk very well. But sometimes he's his old rascally self. Devin?"

Devin's eyes looked heavy, glaucous, but they sharpened on Yuki.

"Mr. Richter, there's someone here to see you," the nurse said.

Devin stared hard at Yuki, and she was suddenly frightened. The night of the rape flooded her. His eyes, though clouded, were the same she'd seen above her. She closed her eyes and shook her head to clear it, then took a deep breath, opened her eyes, stronger now. "I came a long way to see you, Devin. I'm dying."

Devin moved his mouth but only a stuttered grunt came out, and Yuki saw muscles and tendons in his neck straining.

"I'll leave you two alone. If you need one of us, just press the button on the side of the bed." The receptionist left the room, letting the door click shut.

Yuki turned back to Devin. "Do you know who I am?"

Devin continued to stare, then he nodded his head, and Yuki felt her lips tighten.

"You're one of them." He sounded like he had a mouth full of gum, and Yuki had to strain to understand him. "It was...was a long time ago." He coughed into his fist, leaving a gob of saliva on his hand. It shone quietly in the silver light entering through the slats of a metal blind.

Yuki said nothing.

"Japs. In that camp."

"Yes. Good. You remember. I was in the camp."

"I taught them how to play ball. It's big over there now. In Japan."

Yuki stared at him, waiting for the realization of who she was to hit, wondering if it would. Maybe he'd forgotten the entire incident.

"In Japan." He coughed again. "Th...they're good players. Some play in the states now."

"Do you remember me?"

He squinted at her. "The...there were a lot of kids that played ball there. But they were all boys. Not like today. My granddaughter plays baseball."

"What else do you remember about the camp?"

"It was war. I just did my job."

Was there a hint of indignance in his voice? Yuki bristled. "This has nothing to do with playing ball. You raped me. You and Larry Voyce."

Devin wheezed, then said, "Larry's dead."

"You should be dead!" Yuki yelled. "You should die for what you did."

Devin stared down at his robe, saying nothing. Then his head came up and he met Yuki's eyes. "I never meant to do that. I was drunk. It was Larry's idea."

"That doesn't make it right."

"I never said it was right."

"Fuck you! You took a piece of life away from that little girl."

Tears started to flow from his eyes unabated. "I can't give it back to her."

"You can take responsibility." Yuki pulled the gun out of her purse, balanced it in her hand momentarily, then placed it on the small table next to the bed.

"Kill me if you want. I do...don't care if I die." Devin glanced at the gun, then looked away, then back at Yuki.

"I don't either," replied Yuki.

"Wh...what do you want from me?" His voice garbled again, and saliva streamed out the corners of his open mouth. he was taking deep breaths now, gulping air.

"You could start with an apology."

He looked down, first at the blanket, then at the gun.

Yuki saw a stain in the sheet where he'd wet himself.

"I'm sorry. I was drunk. I didn't mean it. If I could undo it I would."

Yuki realized this must be the story he told himself, his grand excuse. "I was a little girl then. Twelve. In spite of the camp, the displacement, the rules, bad food, curfews, I was almost happy. My life stretched before me like the fields outside camp." She didn't realize the tears starting to slip down her cheeks, didn't realize how she kept talking, circling like a bird searching a roost, until she was talking about it, telling him what he'd done as she remembered it.

And then it was finished and she was finished. She gazed at Devin Richter. The man she'd been trying to escape her entire life. His head was bent as if in prayer, and his shoulders shook. He finally raised his head. There were tears on his cheeks, but his dark eyes were now mysteriously clear, and he offered them to Yuki. And in them Yuki saw deep sorrow flowing like a river.

"Hardly a day goes by when I don't think of that. Of you." He stopped and awkwardly scratched his chin, smearing saliva and tears. "I, I always watched you after that, wondering if you'd tell. Wondering why you didn't." He gasped, then reached his arm toward her, passing over the gun, his arm trembling erratically. "I never forgot."

"I never forgot, either. How could you do that to a little girl?"

"You want to kill me?"

Yuki didn't answer. Her emotions stormed.

"God will never forgive me. I've tried."

Yuki said nothing.

"You've lived in hell," he sputtered. He was shaking harder, and through his tears she could hear words, but they weren't enough. Devin's words no longer meant anything.

Yuki stood abruptly. "I've done what I came here to do," she said. "Now it's up to you to make it right." She walked out of the room closing the door firmly behind her.

A few minutes later Yuki pushed the front door open and released herself into the parking lot. Mist rose as hot sun burned the damp asphalt, and grackles chattered noisily in the border of pyracantha, As she walked across the mist, she heard what sounded like a car backfiring and shuddered. She got into the rental car and started it. Driving out of the parking lot she felt weightless.

She didn't remember the driving, entering and exiting the freeway, taking the road toward the canyon's rim. None of it. She did remember walking, staggering and reaching out blindly before she fell. The pain of it was no greater or less than other pain. It carried her now. She thought of Devin and wondered if she'd forgiven him. Then she passed out.

An indefinite time later she woke, lying where she fell, her face crushed into broken lava rock, the mineral tang of it overpowering her. Below her, the gorge where the Snake River roared, fighting the canyon walls that constricted it. The roar of water became the union of all the voices she'd ever heard. It flooded her. She felt her spirit lift, her body tug at it to come back.

When Yuki woke again, she managed to roll onto her back, and the brightness of the sky and the brightness of her pain merged. Her lips were crusted with spittle and powdered rock. She wiped at her face and her hand came back streaked with blood. A meadowlark's call severed the water's roar, leaving momentary silence, then the roar returned.

She remembered one day shortly after she'd arrived at the camp, walking out toward the fence far-flung across a meadow, toward the northern mountains. It was summer and the grasses had been mowed to stubble. Suddenly in front of her a massive flock of blackbirds lifted into the huge sky, and she felt herself lifting with them, but fear entered her and she fell back to earth, to the camp. Now she was there again, walking, feeling the prick of stubbled grass on her bare feet, the bright air on her skin, and again the birds came, swooping over her and lifting as a massive wing into the sky, and this time she joined them.

Acknowledgements

Thanks to Joan Piper, Frank Haulgren, and Dan and Susan Hahn for early reads and valuable suggestions. Special thanks to Chuck Luckmann, Tim Pilgrim, Sara Stamey, Wendy Gorski, and Sherwood Smith for close reads, edits, and valuable suggestions. All of these people helped to make the novel significantly stronger. And a big thanks to Maya Bohnhoff for the cover design, and Jennifer Stevenson and Marissa Doyle for formatting assistance.

About the Author

Paul S. Piper is the author of the novel *The Wolves of Mirr*, and four books of poetry. He lives in Bellingham, Washington with his wife Joan, two cats, Athena and Artemos, and his malamute/huskie hybrid, Django.

About Book View Café

Book View Café is a professional authors' publishing cooperative with authors from all genres including mystery, romance, fantasy, and science fiction.

Readers can enjoy high-quality DRM-free ebooks from their favorite authors at a reasonable price, with select print editions available.

Authors can enjoy earning 90% of the proceeds of each book sold.

Book View Café authors include New York Times and USA Today bestsellers, Nebula, Hugo, Lambda, Chanticleer, National Reader's Choice, and Philip K. Dick Award winner, World Fantasy, Kirkus, and RITA Award nominees, and winners and nominees of many other publishing awards.

To keep informed of new releases, specials, and other news, sign up for Book View Café's monthly newsletter at https://www.bookviewcafe.com/

BOOK VIEW CAFE